THIS BOOK BELONGS TO

Britt-andrea-Paige

Grandpa
Grandma.   '96

*Behind him at a table sat the Dodger and Charley Bates; they
were playing cards with another member of the gang.*

OLIVER TWIST

OLIVER TWIST

Charles Dickens

CONTENTS

LIST OF PLATES

1

In the Workhouse

Oliver Twist was born in a workhouse; and on the day that he was born his poor young mother died.

"She was a good-looking girl," said the doctor, pausing by the bedside. "Where did she come from?"

But nobody knew.

"She was brought here last night," said the pauper woman who had acted as nurse. "She was found lying in the street. She had walked some distance, for her shoes were worn to pieces; but where she came from, or where she was going, nobody knows."

Then the woman took Oliver out of the blanket in which he had been rolled, and dressed him in the old calico robes that had grown yellow from long service; for dozens of babies born in the work-house had worn them too.

Oliver cried lustily. If he could have known that his mother was dead, and that he was born in a workhouse, perhaps he would have cried louder.

The parish authorities sent him to a branch workhouse, three miles off—a baby farm, where an old woman named Mrs Mann took charge of him, for sevenpence-halfpenny a week.

There he rolled about the floor with twenty or thirty other workhouse babies like himself, with not too much to eat, and very little to wear. Only the strongest babies lived to grow up at Mrs Mann's.

But there was a sturdy spirit in Oliver's breast, and, notwithstanding the meagre food and scant clothing, Oliver lived to be nine years old; and he was spending his ninth birthday in the coal cellar with two other boys, who had been locked up there with him, after a sound thrashing from Mrs Mann, because they had actually complained that they were hungry.

Mrs Mann had just drawn the bolt of the cellar door when she was startled to see Mr Bumble—the beadle of the workhouse where Oliver was born—trying to undo the latch of the garden gate.

"Goodness gracious! Is that you, Mr Bumble, sir?" said Mrs Mann, thrusting her head out of the window. And then she whispered to the girl who helped her, "Susan, take Oliver and them two other brats upstairs, and wash 'em directly. My heart alive! Mr Bumble, how glad I am to see you, surely."

Now Mr Bumble was a fat man, and easily angered, and he gave the little wicket gate a tremendous shake, and then bestowed upon it a kick.

The three boys had been taken out of the cellar by this time, and Mrs Mann ran into the garden crying, "To think that I should have forgot that the gate was bolted on the inside on account of them dear children! Walk in, sir. Walk in, pray, Mr Bumble. Do, sir," and she curtsied humbly.

But that did not pacify the beadle; for Mr Bumble in his cocked hat, swinging his cane, thought himself a very important individual indeed.

He asked Mrs Mann haughtily if she thought it respectable conduct to keep parish officers waiting at the gate, when they came on parish business.

"I am sure, Mr Bumble, I was only a-telling the dear children, as is so fond of you, that it was you a-coming," said Mrs Mann.

"Well, well, Mrs Mann," replied the beadle in a calmer tone; for he was gratified at her humility, "it may be as you say; it may be. Lead the way, Mrs Mann, for I am come on business, and have something to say."

Mrs Mann ushered him into a small parlour with a brick floor, and officiously put his cocked hat and cane on the table before him, and begged him in her sweetest manner to have a little drop of something.

"Not a drop," said Mr Bumble, "not a drop!" and he waved his right hand in a dignified way.

"Just a leetle drop, with a little cold water, and a lump of sugar," persuaded Mrs Mann.

At that Mr Bumble coughed, and consented to have some gin, which Mrs Mann told him she kept in the house for "the blessed infants" when they were ill.

"And now about business," said Mr Bumble, after he had drunk her health; and taking out a leather pocket-book, he added: "The child that was baptized Oliver Twist is nine years old today. And notwithstanding an offered reward of ten pound, which was afterwards increased to twenty pound, we have never been able to discover who his father is, or what was his mother's name."

"How comes he to have any name at all, then?" asked Mrs Mann.

The beadle drew himself up with great pride, and said, "I invented it."

"You, Mr Bumble?"

"I, Mrs Mann. We name our foundlings in reg'lar alphabet order. The last was S,—Swubble, I named him. This was a T,—Twist, I named *him*. The next one that comes will be Unwin, and the next Vilkins. I have got names ready made to the end of the alphabet, and all the way through it again, when we come to Z."

"Why, you're quite a lit'rary character, sir!" said Mrs Mann.

"Well, well," said the beadle, "perhaps I may be. Perhaps I may be, Mrs Mann." Then he finished the gin and water, and added that Oliver being now too old to remain at the baby farm, the managers had determined to have him back into the House. "I have come out myself to take him there," said Mr Bumble. "So let me see him at once."

"I'll fetch him directly," said Mrs Mann; and she left the room for that purpose.

Susan had given Oliver's face and hands a hasty wash, and Mrs Mann brought him into the room, saying, "Make a bow to the gentleman."

"Will you go along with me, Oliver?" said Mr Bumble in a majestic voice.

Oliver had had more cuffs than ha'pence—as the saying is—at Mrs Mann's, and he did not object to leaving her at all. He was going to say, "Yes," immediately, when he looked up and caught sight of Mrs Mann behind the beadle's chair, shaking her fist at him, and frowning furiously.

"Will she go with me?" asked poor Oliver, taking the hint at once.

"No, she can't," said Mr Bumble. "But she'll come to see you sometimes."

At that Oliver tried to cry, but he was so hungry, that he ended by crying quite naturally; whereupon Mrs Mann kissed him immediately, and gave him some bread-and-butter lest he might seem too hungry when he reached the workhouse.

And then she put his little brown cloth parish cap on his head, and Mr Bumble took him away to the old workhouse where he was born, and there he had another piece of bread-and-butter before Mr Bumble conducted him into a large whitewashed room, where eight or ten fat gentlemen were sitting round a table.

They were the managers of the workhouse, and after having asked Oliver his name, they told him that as he had no father or mother or anybody belonging to him, he was to be educated there, and taught a useful trade.

Life at the workhouse was not any better than at Mrs Mann's, and there was not much more to eat—for in those days the condition of workhouses was very poor; one boy, indeed, got so ravenous at last that he hinted darkly to his companions that unless he had something more to eat he was afraid he would wake up so hungry some night that he would eat the boy that slept next him. And as he was a tall fellow, with a wild and hungry eye, they were half afraid that he would.

So a council was held, and lots were cast as to who should walk up to the master after supper that evening, and ask for more; and the lot fell on Oliver Twist.

The boys were fed in a large stone hall, with a copper at the end in which the gruel was cooked. The evening arrived; and the boys took their places. The master took his station at the copper—with two old pauper women to help him—and ladled out the gruel into basins. Each boy was allowed one basin, and no more.

The boys swallowed it ravenously; it soon disappeared, and then they whispered and winked at Oliver, and those sitting next him nudged him.

Oliver rose from his seat. It was a bold thing to do; but he was desperate with hunger, and, advancing to the master with his basin in his hand, he said tremulously: "Please, sir, I want some more."

The master was a fat, healthy man, but he turned pale from astonishment, and clung to the copper for support; the old pauper women looked thunderstruck; the boys were paralysed with fear.

"What?" said the master at last.

"Please, sir, I want some more."

The master aimed a blow at Oliver's head with the ladle; then he held him by the arms, and shouted for the beadle.

Mr Bumble came rushing in. Hearing what the matter was, he turned pale himself, and then tore into the big whitewashed room where the managers were sitting, and gasped:

"Oliver Twist has asked for more!"

Then there was a tremendous fuss. Oliver was confined in a dark and solitary room, and the next morning a bill was pasted on the outside of the gate, offering a reward of five pounds to anybody who would take him off the hands of the parish and apprentice him to a trade.

For one week Oliver remained a close prisoner, except when he was taken out to the stone hall to be whipped in public as a warning to the other boys. And then one morning a chimney sweep passed that way, and read the bill on the gate.

"Wo-o!" said the chimney sweep to his donkey, and gave it a

blow on the head. He had a cruel face. He gave the donkey's jaw a wrench, and then he read the bill again, and then he smiled. He owed five pounds to his landlord, and he fancied he saw a very easy way of paying it.

One of the managers—a fat gentleman in a white waistcoat—happened to be standing at the gate. "This here boy, sir," said the chimney sweep, addressing him, "wot the parish wants to 'prentice."

"What of him?" asked the gentleman in the white waistcoat.

"If the parish would like him to learn a light, pleasant trade in a good 'spectable chimney sweeping bisness, I want a 'prentice, and am ready to take him!"

"Walk in," said the gentleman in the white waistcoat. And he took the chimney sweep into the room where the other managers were sitting.

"It's a nasty trade," said one gentleman, when he had heard what the chimney sweep wanted.

"Young boys have been smothered in chimneys before now," said another.

For in those days chimneys were not swept with long-handled brushes as they are swept now. Young boys climbed up the chimneys, scraping down the soot as they went.

"It's such a nasty business," put in another gentleman, "that you ought to take something less than the premium we offer."

So, after a good deal of bargaining on both sides, the chimney sweep agreed to take Oliver for three pounds ten shillings.

Then Oliver was taken out of the dark room, and a clean shirt was given him to put on, and Mr Bumble—the beadle—brought him a basin of gruel and a piece of bread, and told him pompously that he was going to be made "a 'prentice of."

"A 'prentice, sir?" asked the poor little boy, trembling.

"Yes, Oliver," said the beadle. "The kind and blessed gentlemen which is so many parents to you, Oliver, when you have none of your own, are going to 'prentice you, and to set you up in life, and make a man of you, although the expense to the parish is three pound ten!—three pound ten, Oliver!—seventy shillings!—one hundred and forty sixpences!—and all for a naughty orphan which nobody can't love.

The tears rolled down poor Oliver's cheeks. He sobbed bitterly.

"Wipe your eyes with the cuffs of your jacket," said Mr Bumble, "and don't cry into your gruel. That's a very foolish action, Oliver."

Oliver did as he was bid. And then Mr Bumble told him that he was to appear before the magistrates where the agreement that was to apprentice him to the chimney sweep was to be signed, and that if the gentlemen asked him if he wanted to be apprenticed he was to say, "Yes," immediately.

Oliver followed the beadle, with a beating heart, into a large room where two old gentlemen with powdered heads sat behind a desk.

They were the magistrates, and the agreement would have to be approved of by them before the managers could hand Oliver over to be apprenticed.

One was reading a newspaper, and the other was looking at the agreement through a pair of tortoiseshell spectacles. One of the managers was standing in front of the desk, on one side; and the chimney sweep, with a dirty, evil-looking face, on the other.

After Oliver was introduced and had made his bow, the magistrate with the tortoiseshell spectacles said, "I suppose he's fond of chimney sweeping."

"Please, sir, I want some more."

"He dotes on it, your worship," said Mr Bumble, giving Oliver a sly pinch to intimate that he had better not say he did not.

"And he will be a sweep, will he?" inquired the old gentleman.

"If we was to bind him to any other trade tomorrow, he'd run away direct, your worship," replied Bumble.

Oliver was too much frightened to speak. He was looking at the cruel face of his future master, and grew more frightened than ever.

"And this man that's to be his master—you, sir—you'll treat him well, and feed him, and do all that sort of thing, will you?" said the old gentleman.

"When I says I will, I means I will," said the chimney sweep doggedly.

The old gentleman took up his pen to sign the agreement, when his eyes suddenly encountered the terrified face of the poor little boy, looking at the chimney sweep with fear and horror.

He put down his pen, leaned over the desk, and stared at Oliver. "My boy!" he said, so kindly that Oliver started, trembled violently, and burst into tears.

"My boy!" repeated the old gentleman, "you look pale and frightened. What is the matter?"

"Stand away from him, Beadle," said the other magistrate, laying aside the paper, and leaning forward with an expression of interest. "Now, boy, tell us what is the matter. Don't be afraid."

Then Oliver fell on his knees, and, clasping his hands together, prayed the magistrates to starve, or beat, or kill him, rather than send him away with that cruel-looking man.

"Well," exclaimed Mr Bumble, "of all the artful and designing orphans that I ever see, Oliver, you are one of the most barefacedest!"

"Hold your tongue, Beadle," said the magistrate

Which so astonished Mr Bumble, that he asked, "Did your worship speak to me?"

"Yes," said the magistrate again. "Hold your tongue."

Then the gentleman in the tortoiseshell spectacles nodded to the other magistrate, and, tossing aside the agreement on the desk, said, "We refuse to sign these papers."

And the other magistrate added sharply, "Take the boy back to the workhouse, and treat him kindly. He seems to want it."

The next morning the bill was put up on the gate again, offering five pounds to anybody who would take Oliver off the hands of the parish.

2

At Mr Sowerberry's

The managers then came to the conclusion that the best thing would be to send Oliver to sea. And Mr Bumble was sent round to inquire whether any ship captain wanted a cabin-boy.

The beadle was on his way home to the workhouse after one of these jaunts, when he met at the gate Mr Sowerberry, the undertaker.

He was a tall, gaunt man dressed in seedy black clothes, with darned cotton stockings of the same colour, and shoes to answer, and he said, shaking Mr Bumble by the hand, "I have taken the measure of the two women who died last night, Mr Bumble."

"You'll make your fortune, Mr Sowerberry," said the beadle taking a pinch of snuff from a little box in the shape of a coffin, which the undertaker held out to him.

"Think so?" said Mr Sowerberry.

"By-the-bye, you don't know anybody that wants a boy, do you?" asked Mr Bumble. "Liberal terms, Mr Sowerberry;" and he pointed to the bill on the gate, and gave three distinct raps upon the words, "five pounds."

"Gadso!" said the undertaker. "That's the very thing I have been meaning to speak with you about; I think I should like to take the boy myself."

So Mr Bumble took him by the arm, and led him into the workhouse. And after a little talk with the managers, it was agreed that Oliver should be sent on trial to the undertaker's, as house-boy, that very evening.

Oliver took the news in silence; and with a shirt and a pair of socks tied up in a brown-paper parcel in his hand, he was led away by Mr Bumble.

Mr Bumble carried his head very erect, as a beadle always should. And as they neared their destination, he happened to look down to see that Oliver was in good order to be received by his new master.

"Oliver!" said Mr Bumble.

"Yes, sir," said the child in a low, tremulous voice.

"Pull that cap off your eyes, and hold up your head, sir."

Oliver did so. And then Mr Bumble saw that tears were rolling down the boy's cheeks.

The beadle looked at him sternly. It only made the tears come faster. And withdrawing his other hand from Mr Bumble's, he covered his face with both, and wept bitterly.

"Well!" exclaimed Mr Bumble. "Of all the ungratefullest, and worst-disposed boys as ever I see, Oliver, you are the . . ."

"No, no, sir," sobbed Oliver, clinging to Mr Bumble's hand. "No, no, sir; I will be good indeed. Indeed, indeed I will, sir. I am a very little boy, sir, and it is so—so . . ."

"So what?" inquired the beadle in amazement.

"So lonely, sir! So very lonely. Everybody hates me. Oh! sir, don't, pray don't be cross to me!" The child beat his hand on his heart, and looked up at the beadle's face in agony.

Mr Bumble stared in astonishment for a moment. Then something in the forlorn little boy's face made him cough a husky cough; he could not answer for a moment. Then he told Oliver to be a good boy, and walked along in silence.

The undertaker had just put up the shutters of his shop, and was writing by the light of a dismal candle when the newcomers entered. And Mr Bumble told Oliver to make a bow.

"Oh! that's the boy, is it?" said the undertaker, lifting the candle above his head to get a better view. "Mrs Sowerberry, will you have the goodness to come here, my dear?"

A little thin woman with a vixenish face came out of the room behind the shop.

"My dear," said Mr Sowerberry, "this is the boy from the workhouse that I told you of."

Oliver bowed again.

"Dear me," said Mrs Sowerberry, "he's very small."

"Why, he *is* rather small," said Mr Bumble, looking at Oliver as if it were Oliver's own fault that he was no bigger. "He *is* small. But he'll grow, Mrs Sowerberry—he'll grow."

"Ah! I daresay he will," replied Mrs Sowerberry pettishly—"on our victuals and our drink. I see no saving in parish children—not I; for they always cost more to keep than they are worth. However, men always think they know best. There! get downstairs, little bag o'bones." And, opening a side door, she pushed Oliver down a flight of dark stairs into a stone-floor kitchen, where sat a slatternly girl with shoes down at heel, and big holes in her blue worsted stockings.

"Here, Charlotte," said Mrs Sowerberry, "give this boy some of the cold bits that were put by for Trip. He hasn't come home since the morning, so he may go without 'em. I daresay the boy isn't too dainty to eat them. Are you, boy?"

Oliver said, "No," eagerly. His eyes were glistening at the sight of meat; and he sat down before the plateful of coarse broken food that had been kept for the dog, and fell upon it like a starving wolf.

Mrs Sowerberry gazed at him in horror. "Well!" she exclaimed. "Have you done?"

There being nothing more left to eat on the plate, Oliver was obliged to say, "Yes."

"Then come with me," said Mrs Sowerberry, taking up a dim and dirty lamp, and leading the way upstairs. "Your bed is under the counter. You don't mind sleeping among the coffins, I suppose? But it don't much matter whether you do or you don't, for you can't sleep anywheres else."

Oliver meekly followed his new mistress. And there in the shop, under the counter, she showed him his bed, and left him to himself Oliver put the lamp on a workman's bench, and gazed timidly round the shop. A half-finished coffin on black trestles stood in the middle, and on the wall hung a large picture of a hearse drawn by four black steeds. Oliver tried not to look at the coffin, but his eyes persisted in wandering towards it; and every time he looked at it, he could fancy a dead body lying in it, and almost expected to see it slowly rear its head to drive him mad with fear.

The shop was close and hot, and bright-headed nails and shreds of black cloth littered the floor. He fancied the flock mattress under the counter looked like a grave.

He felt alone in a strange place; and though he had no friends to care for, or any who cared for him, yet his heart was heavy, and he wished, as he crept into bed, that he was lying in the churchyard ground, with the tall grass waving gently above his head, and the sound of the old deep bell to soothe him in his sleep.

A loud kicking at the outside of the shop door awoke him next morning. He jumped up, and began to huddle on his clothes, the kicking going on all the time. But as soon as he began to undo the chain, the kicking stopped, and a voice shouted:

"Open the door, will yer?"

"I will directly, sir," said Oliver, beginning to turn the key.

Then the voice said through the keyhole, "I suppose yer the new boy, ain't yer?"

"Yes, sir," said Oliver.

"How old are yer?"

"Ten, sir."

"Then I'll whop yer when I get in; you just see if I don't, my workhus brat!" And the person on the other side of the door whistled.

Oliver drew back the bolts with a trembling hand, and opened the door. And then he saw, sitting on a post in front of the house, a big charity boy eating a slice of bread-and-butter, which he cut with a clasp knife.

"I beg your pardon, sir," said Oliver. "Did you knock?"

"I kicked," replied the charity boy.

"Did you want a coffin, sir?" asked Oliver innocently.

This made the charity boy very angry, for he thought Oliver was making fun of him. "Yer don't know who I am, I suppose, Workhus?" said he, climbing down from the post.

"No, sir," said Oliver.

"I'm Mister Noah Claypole; and you're under me. Take down the shutters, yer idle young ruffian;" and the charity boy gave him a kick.

He was a big, lumbering youth, with a heavy countenance. His eyes were small, and his nose was red, and he had on yellow breeches.

Oliver took down one shutter, but it was so heavy that in his effort to lift it, he broke a pane of glass. Noah had to come to his help with the others, and he told him "he'd catch it."

And Mr and Mrs Sowerberry coming in soon after, Oliver did "catch it," as Noah had said. Then the two went down the flight of dark stairs to breakfast in the kitchen.

"Come near the fire, Noah," said Charlotte. "I've saved a nice little bit of bacon for you from Master's breakfast. Oliver, shut that door at Mister Noah's back, and take them bits that I've put on the cover of the bread-pan. There's your tea; take it away to that box and drink it there, and make haste, for they'll want you to mind the shop. D'ye hear?"

"D'ye hear, Workhus?" said the charity boy.

"Lor', Noah," said Charlotte, "why don't you leave the boy alone?"

"Let him alone," said Noah. "Why, everybody lets him alone for the matter of that. Neither his father nor his mother will ever interfere with him. All his relations let him have his own way, pretty well. He! he! he!"

Charlotte laughed, and they both looked contemptuously at Oliver—as he sat shivering in the coldest corner of the room, and ate the stale pieces that had been put aside for him.

Noah was not a workhouse orphan like poor Oliver, who knew nothing of his parents. Noah's drunken father and mother lived in the town, although he had been brought up on charity. And as the shop boys in the streets called out "Charity" after Noah, the charity boy thought it a fine thing to hurl "Workhus!" at the helpless little orphan that did not know even his father's name.

Oliver had been about three weeks at the undertaker's, when it struck Mr Sowerberry that the boy—with his pale, handsome face, and melancholy air—would make a capital mute, or mourner, to attend at children's funerals; so by-and-by Oliver was promoted to attend the funerals, carrying a black stick, and wearing a hat-band. This made Noah furiously jealous, and he treated Oliver worse than ever, calling him unceasingly a "workhus brat."

One day Oliver and Noah had just sat down to dinner, when Charlotte was called away. Noah immediately put his feet on the table-cloth, pulled Oliver's hair, and called him a sneak.

"Workhus," said Noah, "how's your mother?"

"She's dead," said Oliver, colouring and breathing quickly. "Don't you say anything about her to me." His mouth quivered. Noah thought he would goad him into tears.

"What did she die of, Workhus?"

"Of a broken heart, one of the old nurses told me," said Oliver. And he added, half to himself, with tears in his eyes, "I think I know what it must be to die of that."

"Tol de rol lol lol, right fol lairy, Workhus," said Noah, delighted. "What's set you snivelling now?"

"Not you," replied Oliver, hastily brushing the tears away. "Don't think it."

"Oh, not me, eh?" sneered Noah.

"No, not you. There, that's enough. Don't say anything more to me about my mother," said Oliver sharply. "You'd better not."

"Better not! Workhus, don't be impudent. Your mother, too. She was a nice 'un, she was. Oh, lor'!—and Noah curled up his red nose, and nodded his head knowingly.

"Yer know, Workhus," continued Noah, in a jeering tone of pretended pity, "it can't be helped now; and of course you couldn't help it then; and I'm very sorry for it; and I'm sure we all are, and pity yer very much. But yer must know, Workhus, yer mother was a right down bad 'un."

"What did you say?" said Oliver quickly.

"A regular right down bad 'un. And it's a great deal better, Workhus, that she died, or else she'd have been transported or hung."

Crimson with fury, Oliver started up, seized Noah by the throat, shook him till his teeth chattered in his head; and, collecting his whole force into one heavy blow, felled him to the ground.

The boy's spirit was roused at last. No one looking at him now could imagine him to be the quiet, mild, dejected child that harsh treatment had made him. The cruel insult to his dead mother had set his blood on fire. His breast heaved; he held up his head; his eye was bright as he stood glaring over his cowardly tormentor, who now lay crouching at his feet.

"He'll murder me!" blubbered Noah. "Charlotte!—Missus!— Here's the new boy a-murdering of me! Help! Help! Oliver's gone mad!—Charlotte!"

He was answered by a loud scream from Charlotte, and a louder scream from Mrs Sowerberry. Charlotte rushed into the kitchen, and seized Oliver with her utmost force. "Oh, you little wretch!" she screamed. And then with a blow from her big fist between each word, "Oh—you—little—ungrateful—murderous—horrid—villain!"

Mrs Sowerberry plunged in, and beat him too. And the valiant Noah rose from the ground and pummelled him behind.

Then they dragged Oliver, struggling and shouting, into the coal cellar, and there locked him up.

"Oh, Charlotte!"—and Mrs Sowerberry burst out crying—"what a mercy we have not all been murdered in our beds."

"A mercy, indeed, ma'am," replied Charlotte. "I only hope Master will not bring any more of them dreadful creatures here. Poor Noah! He was all but killed, ma'am, when I come in."

And the big charity boy, who was a head and shoulders taller than Oliver, rubbed his eyes and performed some affecting tears and sniffs.

Meanwhile, Oliver was making vigorous plunges at the door of the coal cellar, kicking it furiously.

"What's to be done?" exclaimed Mrs Sowerberry.

"Your master's not at home; there's not a man in the house, and he'll kick the door down in ten minutes."

"Dear, dear! I don't know, ma'am," said Charlotte, "unless we send for the police officers."

"Or the millingtary," suggested Noah.

"No, no," said Mrs Sowerberry. "Run to Mr Bumble, Noah, and tell him to come directly. Never mind your cap! Make haste. You can hold a knife to that black eye as you run along. It'll keep the swelling down."

Noah started off at his fullest speed, tearing through the streets pell-mell with a clasp knife at his eye; and, knocking at the gate of the workhouse, burst into the yard, shrieking, "Mr Bumble! Mr Bumble!"

Mr Bumble happened to be in the yard.

"Oh, Mr Bumble, sir!" cried Noah; "Oliver has—Oliver has . . ."

"Not run away?" asked Mr Bumble. "He hasn't run away, has he, Noah?"

'No, sir, no. Not run away, sir, but he's turned vicious," said Noah. "He tried to murder me; and then he tried to murder Charlotte; and then Missus. Oh! what a dreadful pain it is! Such agony, please, sir!" and Noah writhed and twisted his body into all sorts of shapes.

At that moment one of the managers—the gentleman in the white waistcoat—crossed the yard, and angrily inquired what Noah was howling for.

"It's a poor boy from the charity school, sir," replied Mr Bumble, "who has been nearly murdered by young Oliver Twist. And," added the beadle, with a face of ashy paleness, "he has likewise attempted to murder the female servant."

"And his missus," put in Noah Claypole.

"And his master, too, I think you said, Noah?" added Mr Bumble.

"No, Mr Sowerberry was out, or he would have murdered him," replied Noah. "He said he wanted to."

"Ah! said he wanted to, did he, my boy?" said the gentleman in the white waistcoat.

"Yes, sir," replied Noah. "And please, sir, Missus wants to know whether Mr Bumble can spare time to step up there, directly, and flog Oliver—'cause Master's out."

"Bumble," said the gentleman in the white waistcoat, "just you step up to Sowerberry's with your cane, and see what's best to be done. Don't spare him, Bumble."

"No, I will not, sir," replied the beadle; and he proceeded imme-

diately to the scene of action, where Oliver was still kicking vigor-
ously at the cellar door.

Mrs Sowerberry and Charlotte gave such an alarming account of
Oliver's fierceness, that the beadle judged it prudent to let Oliver
know who was outside the door before he opened it. So he put his
mouth to the keyhole, and said in a deep, impressive voice,
"Oliver!"

"Come; you let me out!" replied Oliver from the inside.

"Do you know this here voice, Oliver?" said Mr Bumble.

"Yes," replied Oliver.

"Ain't you afraid of it, sir? Ain't you a-trembling while I speak,
sir?"

"No," replied Oliver boldly.

Mr Bumble was staggered. He stepped back from the keyhole;
drew himself up to his full height, and looked from one to another
of the three bystanders in mute astonishment.

"Oh, you know, Mr Bumble, he must be mad," said Mrs
Sowerberry. "No boy in half his senses would venture to speak so to
you."

"It is not Madness, ma'am," replied Mr Bumble, after a few moments of deep thought; "it's Meat!"

"Meat!" exclaimed Mrs Sowerberry.

"Meat, ma'am, meat. You've overfed him, ma'am. If you had
kept the boy on gruel, ma'am, this would never have happened."

"Dear! dear!" ejaculated Mrs Sowerberry, piously raising her
eyes to the ceiling. "This comes of being liberal!" And Mrs
Sowerberry's liberality had consisted in giving to Oliver all the
scraps which nobody else would eat.

"The only thing now that can be done," said Mr Bumble, "is to leave him in the cellar for a day or two, till he's a little starved down; and then to take him out, and keep him on gruel all through his apprenticeship."

At this moment Mr Sowerberry, who had been away from home, appeared on the scene, and Mrs Sowerberry and Charlotte repeated the story of his assault on Noah, with many additions, in the hope of rousing the undertaker's anger; because, on the whole, Mr Sowerberry had been inclined to be kind generally to Oliver.

The undertaker, hearing the story, opened the cellar door, and dragged his rebellious apprentice out by the collar.

"Now you're a nice young fellow, ain't you?" said Mr Sowerberry, giving him a shake and a box on the ear.

"He called my mother names," replied Oliver, with the flush still on his face and the brightness in his eyes.

"Well, and what if he did?" cried Mrs Sowerberry. "She deserved what he said."

"She didn't," said Oliver.

"She did," said Mrs Sowerberry.

"It's a lie," said Oliver.

Mrs Sowerberry burst into a flood of tears

After that, Mr Sowerberry, although kindly disposed to the boy, was obliged to give him a drubbing, and, for the rest of the day, Oliver was shut up in the back kitchen with nothing more than a slice of bread. And at night Mrs Sowerberry looked into the room, and ordered him upstairs to his dismal bed.

He had not cried when they had beaten him, and he had listened to their taunts with a look of contempt. But now, when he found himself alone in the gloomy workshop, where none could see or hear him, Oliver fell on his knees and cried bitterly.

For a long time he knelt, broken with misery; and when he roused himself, the candle was burning low in the socket. He looked round, and listened intently. There was not a sound. Everybody had gone to bed. And then he gently undid the fastenings of the shop door, and looked out.

It was a cold, dark night; and the stars were shining brightly. He softly reclosed the door, and before the candle flickered out, he tied up in a handkerchief the shirt and socks he had brought from the workhouse, and waited for the day to break.

And with the first ray of light that struggled through the chinks in the shutters, Oliver arose, and again unbarred the door. One timid look around—one moment's pause of hesitation—then he closed the door behind him, and was in the open street.

As he ran along, he presently found himself on a road that led to Mrs Mann's baby farm, where he had lived his first nine years of life. His way lay directly in front of the cottage; and when he thought of that, his heart beat quickly, and he was half inclined to return. But he had come a long way, and it would waste so much time to go back. Besides, it was so early that there was very little fear of his being seen. So on he went, till he reached the cottage.

There was no one about. Oliver stopped, and peeped into the garden. A child was weeding one of the little beds, and as he lifted his pale face, Oliver recognized one of the little boys who had been his friend and playmate. They had been beaten and starved, and shut up together, many and many a time.

"Hush, Dick," said Oliver, as the boy ran to the gate and thrust his thin arm between the rails to greet him. "Is anyone up?"

"Nobody but me," replied the child.

"You mustn't say you saw me, Dick," said Oliver. "I'm running away. They beat and ill-use me, Dick; and I'm going to seek my fortune some long way off. I don't know where. How pale you are!"

"I heard the doctor tell them I was dying," replied the child. "I'm very glad to see you, Oliver. But don't stop, don't stop."

"Yes, yes, I will, to say goodbye to you," said Oliver. "I shall see you again, Dick. I know I shall. You will be well and happy!"

"I hope so," replied the child. "After I am dead, but not before, Oliver, because I dream so much of Heaven and Angels, and of kind faces that I never see when I am awake. Kiss me," said the child, climbing up the low gate, and flinging his little arms round Oliver's neck. "Goodbye, dear! God bless you!"

It was the first blessing that Oliver had ever heard invoked upon his head. And in all his after-life he never once forgot it.

He saw, sitting on a post, a big charity boy, eating a slice of bread-and-butter which he had cut with a clasp knife.

He waited at the bottom of a steep hill till a stage coach came up.

3

At Fagin's

Oliver started on his way, and by eight o'clock had left the town nearly five miles behind. But he didn't feel safe yet, and still ran on, and hid behind hedges in turn till midday.

Then he sat down to rest by the side of a milestone, and began to wonder where he was to go, and what he was to do for a living.

On the stone was marked "Seventy miles from London." London! Oliver had heard the old men in the workhouse say that no lad of spirit need ever want in London; and that there were ways of living in that vast City that country lads had no idea of.

He jumped up then, and began his tramp again, and, as he went, he wondered how he could ever reach the place. He had a crust of bread tied up with his shirt and socks, and a penny, too, that Mr Sowerberry had given him one day when he had been pleased with him. But what was that to help him on so long a journey in hungry winter time? He ate his crust of bread, and begged for water at the cottage doors. And when the night came, he turned into a meadow, and, creeping close up under a hayrick, he fell asleep through sheer weariness, and forgot his hunger and cold.

He was cold and stiff when he got up next morning, and so hungry that he spent his penny on a small loaf in the very first village he came to. He could not walk much that day. And another night spent in the bleak air made him so weak that he could hardly crawl along.

He waited at the bottom of a steep hill till a stage coach came up, and then begged of the outside passengers; but no one heeded him.

Sometimes when he stopped to beg, people threatened to set the dog on him; and if he showed his nose in a shop, they talked about the beadle.

Indeed, if it had not been for a good-hearted turnpike man, and a benevolent old lady, Oliver must have died upon the road. But the first gave him a meal of bread and cheese; and the old lady gave him food and shelter and money, and sent him away with such kind and gentle words, that they sank deep into Oliver's soul.

Early on the seventh morning after he had left his native place, Oliver limped into the little town of Barnet, and sat down—with bleeding feet, and covered with dust—upon a doorstep.

No one took any notice of him; some just turned their heads and stared, but none relieved him, till he was roused out of his listlessness by observing that a boy, not much more than his own age, was looking earnestly at him from the opposite side of the way.

Oliver did not heed him at first; but the boy kept staring so hard, that at last Oliver lifted his head and returned his steady gaze.

The boy immediately crossed the road, and, going up close to Oliver, said, "Hullo, my covey! What's the row?"

He was one of the queerest-looking boys Oliver had ever seen. He was a dirty, snub-nosed boy, short, with bow legs, and little, sharp, ugly eyes—with all the airs and manners of a man. He wore a man's coat which reached to his heels, with the cuffs turned back half-way up his arms; and his hat was stuck on the top of his head so lightly, that it threatened to fall off every moment, and it would have done so if the wearer had not had a knack of every now and then giving his head a sudden twitch, which brought the hat back to its old place again.

"I'm very hungry and tired," replied Oliver, with tears in his eyes. "I have walked a long way. I have been walking seven days."

"Walking for sivin days! "said the boy. "Oh, I see. Beak's order, eh? But," he added, noticing Oliver's look of surprise, "I s'pose you don't know what a beak is, my flash companion?"

Oliver said he thought it meant a bird's mouth. At which the young gentleman laughed heartily, and told him that a beak meant a magistrate. And after a little more explanation, he said suddenly:

"But, come, you want grub, and you shall have it. I'm at low-water mark myself—only one bob and a magpie; but as far as it goes, I'll fork out and stump. Up with you on your pins."

With that he helped Oliver to rise, and took him to a shop where he bought some ham and bread, and then turned into a public house and ordered a pot of beer; and watched Oliver attentively as he fell upon the food, and, at his new friend's bidding, made a hearty meal.

"Going to London?" asked the strange boy, when Oliver had finished.

"Yes."

"Got any lodgings?"

"No."

"Money?"

"No," repeated Oliver.

The strange boy whistled; and put his arms into his pockets as far as his big coat sleeves would let him.

"Do you live in London?" asked Oliver.

"I do when I'm at home," replied the boy. "I suppose you want some place to sleep in tonight, don't you?"

"I do indeed," said Oliver. "I haven't slept under a roof since I left the country."

"Don't fret your eyelids on that score," said the young gentleman. "I've got to be in London tonight; and I know a 'spectable old genelman as lives there, wot'll give you lodgings for nothink, and never ask for the change—that is, if any genelman he knows interduces you. And don't he know me? Oh no, not in the least! By no means. Certainly not!" And then he smiled, and finished the beer.

After that the two had a confidential talk, the strange boy saying that his name was Jack Dawkins, and that he was known among his intimate friends as "The Artful Dodger." He also spoke highly of the old gentleman who would befriend Oliver, and get him a comfortable place by-and-by.

Oliver was much relieved, and, needless to say, was very willing to go to London with Master Jack Dawkins. It was eleven o'clock when they reached the great City, and, after leading Oliver through all sorts of side streets, they at last turned down a very narrow, dirty, ill-smelling one, full of small shops, and of children crawling in and out of the shop doors. They passed drunken men, and drunken women too, and great ill-looking fellows cautiously emerging from side doors.

Oliver was just wondering whether he had not better run away, when his conductor caught him by the arm, pushed open the door of a house, and drawing him into the passage, closed the door behind them.

The Artful Dodger whistled, and a voice called out, "Now then!"

"Plummy and slam!" returned the Dodger.

This seemed to be a sort of signal that all was right, for a light gleamed in the distance, and a man's face peeped over the banisters.

"There's two on you," said the man. "Who's the t'other one?"

"A new pal," replied the Dodger, pulling Oliver forward.

"Where did he come from?"

"From Greenland," answered the Dodger. "Is Fagin upstairs?"

"Yes," was the reply. "He's sortin' the wipes. Up with you!" The candle was drawn back, and the face disappeared.

Oliver, groping his way with one hand, and having the other firmly grasped by his companion, ascended with much difficulty the dark and broken stairs, and soon they got into a dirty room where a very shrivelled old man with a villainous face—almost hidden in a quantity of matted red hair—was toasting sausages over the fire.

There were a lot of silk handkerchiefs hanging on a clothes-horse; and several rough beds made of old sacks on the floor; and round the table were four or five boys, not any older than the Dodger, smoking long clay pipes.

The Dodger whispered to the man, and all the boys—and the Jew too—turned round and grinned at Oliver.

"This is him, Fagin," said the Dodger. "My friend Oliver Twist."

Fagin shook hands very heartily, and so did the boys.

"We are very glad to see you, Oliver, very," said Fagin. "Dodger, take off the sausages, and draw a tub near the fire for our guest. Ah! I see you're a-staring at the pocket-handkerchiefs, eh, my dear? There are a good many of them, ain't there? We've just looked 'em out, ready for the wash."

At that all the boys laughed boisterously, and soon the whole party sat down to supper. Oliver ate his share, and then Fagin mixed him a glass of hot gin and water, and told him to drink it off directly, as another gentleman wanted the tumbler. Oliver did as he was bid. Immediately he felt himself gently lifted on to one of the sacks; and then he sank into a deep sleep.

Oliver opened his eyes next morning after a long, long sleep. There was no one in the room but Fagin, who was boiling coffee in a saucepan and whistling softly to himself. Oliver was not properly awake. He was in a drowsy state between sleeping and waking, and his eyes closed again just as Fagin turned round and looked at him.

When he opened his eyes again, he saw the Jew take a small box from a trap in the floor, and out of that he took a magnificent gold watch, sparkling with jewels.

"Clever dogs!" muttered Fagin to himself. "Clever dogs! Never peached upon Fagin." And, still muttering to himself, he put the box into its hiding-place, and drew out other boxes from which he took rings, and brooches, and bracelets, and other jewellery; gloating over them as he held each in his hand.

Then he put these away, and took up a tiny trinket, which he had to examine very closely.

Turning suddenly, he saw Oliver's eyes fixed upon him. Fagin shut down the lid of the box with a loud crash. And laying his hand on a bread-knife which was on the table, he started up furiously, trembling with passion. In his terror, Oliver could see the knife quivering in the air.

"What's that? "said Fagin. "What do you watch me for? Why are you awake? What have you seen? Speak out, boy! Quick—quick!—for your life!"

"I wasn't able to sleep any longer, sir," replied Oliver, meekly. "I am very sorry if I have disturbed you, sir."

"You were not awake an hour ago?" said Fagin, scowling fiercely on the boy.

"No! No, indeed!" replied Oliver.

"Are you sure?" cried Fagin, with a still fiercer look than before.

"Upon my word I was not, sir," replied Oliver, earnestly. "I was not indeed, sir."

"Tush, tush, my dear!" said Fagin, resuming his old manner, and toying with the knife a little, as if to show Oliver he had only been in play. "Of course I know that, my dear. I only tried to frighten you. You're a brave boy. Ha, ha! you're a brave boy, Oliver." And he tried to pass it off with a chuckle; but he glanced uneasily at the box as he did so.

"Did you see anything of these pretty things, my dear?" he asked after a pause, laying his hand upon the box.

"Yes, sir," said Oliver.

Fagin turned a little pale. "They're mine, Oliver. My little property. All I have to live on in my old age. The folks call me a miser, my dear. Only a miser—that is all."

Oliver thought he must be a miser. Indeed, to live in such a dirty place when he possessed so many magnificent things. Then he asked if he could get up. And Fagin said, "Certainly," and told him to fetch a pitcher of water from a corner of the room to wash with. "I'll get you a basin," he added.

Oliver got up; walked across the room, and stooped for an

instant to lift the pitcher. When he turned his head, the box was gone.

He had just finished washing, when the Dodger returned with one of the other boys, whom he now introduced as Charley Bates. Then the four sat down to breakfast on the coffee, with some hot rolls and ham which the Dodger had brought home in the crown of his hat.

"Well," said Fagin, glancing slyly at Oliver, and addressing himself to the Dodger, "I hope you've been at work this morning, my dears?"

"Hard," replied the Dodger.

"As nails," added Charley Bates.

"Good boys, good boys," said Fagin. "What have you got, Dodger?"

"A couple of pocket-books," replied that young gentleman.

"Lined?" inquired Fagin with eagerness.

"Pretty well," replied the Dodger, producing two pocket-books—one green, and the other red.

"Not so heavy as they might be," said Fagin, after looking at the inside carefully; "but very neat, and nicely made. Clever workman, ain't he, Oliver?"

"Very, indeed, sir," said Oliver.

At which Charley Bates laughed heartily; very much to the surprise of Oliver, who saw nothing to laugh at in anything that had passed.

"And what have you got, my dear?" said Fagin to Charley Bates.

"Wipes," replied Master Bates; at the same time producing four pocket-handkerchiefs.

"Well," said Fagin, examining them closely, "they're very good ones, very. You haven't marked them well, though, Charley; so the marks shall be picked out with a needle, and we'll teach Oliver how to do it. Shall we, Oliver? Eh? Ha! ha! ha!"

"If you please, sir," said Oliver.

"You'd like to be able to make pocket-handkerchiefs as easy as Charley Bates, wouldn't you, my dear?" said Fagin.

"Very much indeed, sir, if you'll teach me," said Oliver; and this made the two boys laugh still more; Charley Bates adding that Oliver was "jolly green."

When the breakfast was cleared away, the merry old gentleman and the two boys played a curious game. Fagin put a snuff-box in one pocket, a note-case in the other, a diamond pin in his shirt, and a watch in his waistcoat pocket, with a guard chain round his neck, and trotted up and down the room like any old gentleman in the street.

Sometimes he stopped to look into the fire, and sometimes at the door, making-believe that he was staring in at shop windows. At such times he would look constantly round him for fear of thieves, and would slap his pockets in turn to see if he had lost anything, in such a funny and natural manner, that Oliver laughed till the tears ran down his face.

And all the time the two boys followed Fagin about very nimbly, till at last the Dodger trod upon his toes, while Charley Bates stumbled up against him from behind; and in that moment they took from him, with extraordinary rapidity, the snuff-box, note-case, chain, shirt-pin, and pocket-handkerchief.

If Fagin felt a hand in his pocket, he cried out where it was; and then the game began again. They were to take the articles away without his feeling anything.

By-and-by two young women, with rather untidy hair, came to call upon Fagin. One was called Bet, the other Nancy. They were stout, hearty-looking girls, and very free and agreeable in their manners. Fagin gave them each a drink of gin; and by-and-by he gave them money too. And then Charley Bates and the Dodger went out with the girls.

"There, my dear," said Fagin, "that's a pleasant life, isn't it? They have gone out for the day."

"Have they gone to work, sir?" asked Oliver.

"Yes," answered Fagin. And then he added, "Make 'em your models, my dear. Make 'em your models. Do everything they bid you, and take their advice in all matters, especially the Dodger's... Is my handkerchief hanging out of my pocket, my dear?" he asked, stopping short.

"Yes, sir," said Oliver.

"See if you can take it out without my feeling it, as you saw them do when we were at play this morning."

Oliver held up the bottom of the pocket with one hand, as he had seen the Dodger hold it, and drew the handkerchief lightly out of it with the other.

"Is it gone?" cried Fagin.

"Here it is, sir," said Oliver, showing it in his hand.

"You're a clever boy, my dear," said the playful old gentleman, patting Oliver on the head. "I never saw a sharper lad. Here's a shilling for you. And now come here, and I'll show you how to take the marks out of the handkerchiefs."

For many days Oliver remained in Fagin's room picking the marks out of the pocket-handkerchiefs, and sometimes he took part in the old game which Fagin and the boys played regularly.

Oliver often wished to go out with the boys, for he was pining for some fresh air. And at last one morning Fagin let him have his way, and placed him in the care of the Dodger and Charley Bates.

As they went along, Oliver was astonished to find that such steady and hard-working boys behaved so badly in the street. They kept on snatching up an apple or an onion off the corners of the stalls they passed, doing it so quickly, too, that the owners never caught them in the act. They also loitered about the street, instead of hurrying to their work, and Oliver began to think they were not the steady boys Fagin seemed to think they were.

Suddenly, the Dodger drew Charley's attention to an old gentleman who was standing over a bookstall, diligently reading a book that he had picked up.

He was a very respectable-looking personage, with a powdered head and gold spectacles. He was dressed in a bottle-green coat with a black velvet collar; wore white trousers, and carried a smart bamboo cane under his arm.

Charley Bates said he was "a prime plant." And the two boys immediately crossed the road, and slunk close behind the old gentleman.

And then Oliver saw the Dodger put his hand into the old gentleman's pocket, and draw from it a handkerchief. This he handed to Charley Bates, and in a moment away the boys tore, as hard as they could, round the corner.

In an instant the whole mystery of the handkerchiefs, and the watches, and the jewels, and Fagin, was revealed to Oliver. The boys were thieves; and *the work they did was thieving!* With the blood mounting into his face, confused and frightened, Oliver took to his heels. At that very moment the old gentleman, putting his hand into his pocket for his handkerchief, missed it, and, turning, he saw Oliver scudding away as hard as he could.

"Stop thief!" shouted the old gentleman, and made after him with all his might.

As for the Dodger and Charley Bates, they had merely turned into the first doorway round the corner. And when they heard the cry "Stop thief!" and saw Oliver running, they guessed exactly how it had come about, and they also shouted "Stop thief!" and joined in the pursuit.

And soon the cry was taken up by a hundred voices, and pell-mell, helter-skelter tore the people after Oliver. He ran on; terror in his looks; agony in his eyes; large drops of perspiration streaming down his face; till a blow from somebody threw him to the pavement, and the crowd eagerly gathered round.

"Where's the gentleman?" somebody cried.

"Here he is, coming down the street."

"Is this the boy, sir?"

"Yes," said the old gentleman, "I'm afraid it is the boy." And he looked quite sorry that Oliver had been caught.

But before he could say anything more, a policeman made his way through the crowd, and seized Oliver by the collar.

"It wasn't me, indeed, sir. Indeed, indeed, it was two other boys," said Oliver, clasping his hands passionately, and looking round.

"Come, get up," said the policeman, with an ironical laugh.

"Don't hurt him," cried the old gentleman compassionately.

"Oh no, I won't hurt him," said the policeman. And he dragged Oliver away by the collar, while the old gentleman walked by his side, and a crowd of boys followed, shouting triumphantly.

"I would rather not press the case," said the old gentleman anxiously, when they got to the police court. But they told him that the case must go before the magistrate now.

The old gentleman looked quite unhappy when Oliver was locked up, and, turning with a sigh to his book, which had been the innocent cause of all this disturbance, he said to himself, "There is something in that boy's face that touches and interests me. *Can* he be innocent? He looked like... By-the-bye, bless my soul! where have I seen something like that look before?"

After musing for some minutes, he shook his head. "It must be imagination," he said.

And then he read his book again with a troubled countenance, till somebody touched him on the shoulder, and asked him to follow him into the office.

The magistrate sat behind the bar at the upper end; and on one side of the door was a sort of wooden pen in which poor Oliver was standing, trembling at the awfulness of his position.

The magistrate was a bad-tempered man, and listened to what the old gentleman said very impatiently indeed.

As for Oliver, he was so frightened that he could not utter a sound when he was questioned; and he fainted in the court. The bad-tempered magistrate said he knew that the boy was shamming, and committed him to prison with hard labour for three months.

Just then a man came rushing breathlessly into the court, who demanded to be sworn, saying that he had seen it all, and had now come up to speak for Oliver.

He turned out to be the bookstall keeper himself; and he told the magistrate how he had seen two other boys take the handkerchief from the old gentleman's pocket, and how Oliver had run through sheer fright.

"Why didn't you come here before?" asked the magistrate.

"I hadn't a soul to mind the shop," replied the man. "I could get nobody till five minutes ago. I've run all the way."

"Clear the office," shouted the magistrate, dismissing the case.

And when Mr Brownlow—the old gentleman who had been robbed—came out, he saw Oliver Twist lying on the pavement with his shirt unbuttoned, his face deadly white, and a cold tremble convulsing his whole frame.

"Poor boy, poor boy!" said Mr Brownlow, bending over him. "Call a coach, somebody, pray. Directly!"

A coach was got, and Oliver having been carefully laid on one seat, the old gentleman got in and sat himself on the other, and off they drove.

4

Oliver Finds a Friend

The coach rattled away till they stopped at last before a neat house, in a quiet shady street, near Pentonville. Here a bed was prepared by kind hands, in which Oliver was gently laid, and tended with a care that knew no bounds.

But for many days Oliver, tossing with fever, remained insensible to all the goodness of his new friends, till at last he awoke, weak and pallid, from what seemed to have been a long and troubled dream.

"What room is this?" asked Oliver feebly, raising himself on his arm. "This is not the place I went to sleep in."

"Hush, my dear," said a motherly old woman, looking round the curtain. "You must be very quiet, or you'll be ill again. Lie down again, there's a dear!" With these words she gently placed Oliver's head on the pillow, smoothed back his hair, and looked so kindly into his face that he could not help placing his little wasted hand in hers, and drawing it round his neck.

"Save us!" said the old woman, with tears in her eyes. "What a grateful little dear it is! Pretty creetur! What would his mother feel if she had sat by him as I have, and could see him now!"

"Perhaps she does see me," whispered Oliver. "Perhaps she has sat by me. I almost feel as if she had."

"That was the fever, my dear," said the old woman, and she wiped her eyes, brought something for Oliver to drink, and told him to lie very quiet, or he would be ill again.

So Oliver, anxious to please this extraordinarily kind person, lay very quiet indeed, and soon fell into a gentle doze. And when he awoke again, there was a light in the room, and an old gentleman, with a large, loud-ticking gold watch in his hand, was feeling his pulse.

This was the doctor, who spoke very kindly too, and told the old woman—whom he called Mrs Bedwin—to give his patient some tea and dry toast.

In three days' time Oliver was able to sit in an easy-chair, propped up with pillows; and as he was still too weak to walk, Mrs Bedwin had him carried down to her own little room, and Oliver learned that she was Mr Brownlow's housekeeper.

"You're very, very kind to me, ma'am," said Oliver.

"Well, never you mind that, my dear," said the old woman; "that's got nothing to do with your broth. And it's full time you had it, for the doctor says Mr Brownlow may come in to see you this morning; and you must get up your best looks, because the better you look, the more he'll be pleased."

So Oliver drank his broth, and thought he had never tasted anything so good before.

Then Mrs Bedwin asked him if he was fond of pictures; because Oliver was staring so hard at the portrait of a lady hanging on the wall.

"Here, Bull's-eye, mind him, boy! Mind him!"

"I don't know," said Oliver. "I have seen so few that I hardly know. What a beautiful face that lady's is!"

And while they were talking about it, there was a soft rap at the door.

"Come in," said Mrs Bedwin. And in walked Mr Brownlow.

"Poor boy, poor boy!" said Mr Brownlow, unhappy at seeing Oliver so pale and thin. "How do you feel, my dear?"

"Very happy, sir," replied Oliver. "And very grateful indeed, sir, for your goodness to me."

"Poor boy," said Mr Brownlow. "Have you given him any nourishment, Bedwin? Any slops, eh?"

"He has just had a basin of beautiful strong broth, sir," said Mrs Bedwin.

"A couple of glasses of port wine would have done him a great deal more good," returned the old gentleman. And then he cried suddenly, "Why! what's this? Bedwin, look there!"

And he pointed hastily to the picture of the lady Oliver had admired, and then to the boy's face. There was its living copy. The eyes, the head, the mouth—every feature was the same.

Mr Brownlow had cried out so suddenly that it gave Oliver a start, and, being still very weak, he just fainted away. But he soon recovered under Mrs Bedwin's care, and the old gentleman talked to him quietly.

The fainting fit had thrown him back a little, though, and he could not get up to breakfast the next morning. And when he came down again to the housekeeper's room, he was disappointed at seeing that the picture of the beautiful lady had been removed.

But the housekeeper was very kind, and told him all about her own children, who were now grown up; and as Oliver gradually grew better, she began to teach him the game of cribbage. These were very happy days.

When he grew well enough to put on his clothes, Mr Brownlow had a new suit ordered for him, and a new cap, and a new pair of shoes. They were the first brand-new things Oliver had ever possessed.

And now we must go back for a few minutes to the Dodger and Charley Bates. It caused that last-named young gentleman great merriment to think that Oliver had been suspected of being the thief, when he himself had the stolen handkerchief in his own pocket all the time.

But the Artful Dodger put a stop to Master Bates's laughter by asking, "What'll Fagin say?"

"What should he say?" inquired Charley; for the Dodger's manner was very impressive.

Jack Dawkins whistled for answer; scratched his head, and nodded three times. And when he turned on his heel and slunk down the court, Master Bates followed with a thoughtful countenance.

Fagin was sitting over the fire when he heard their feet upon the creaking stairs; and, as he listened, his face changed. "Only two of 'em," he muttered. "Where's the third? They can't have got into trouble."

The footsteps reached the landing. The door was slowly opened, and the Dodger and Charley Bates entered, closing it behind them.

"Where's Oliver?" cried Fagin. "Where's the boy?"

The young thieves looked uneasily at each other.

"What's become of the boy?" repeated Fagin, seizing the Dodger by the collar. "Speak out, or I'll throttle you."

"The traps have got him, and that's all about it," said the Dodger sullenly. "Come, let go of me, will you!" And, swinging himself free, he seized the toasting-fork, and threatened Fagin with it.

Fagin stepped back and seized the pewter pot, and was going to fling it at the Dodger, when Charley Bates set up a terrific howl, and so Fagin flung it at Bates instead of at the Dodger.

"Why, what the blazes is in the wind now?" growled a deep voice at the door. "Who pitched that at me? It's well it's the beer and not the pot as hit me or I'd have settled somebody. Wot's it all about, Fagin? Dash me, if my neck handkercher ain't lined with beer."

The man who growled out these words was a stoutly built fellow of about thirty-five, in a black velveteen coat, dirty drab breeches, laced-up half boots, and grey cotton stockings, which enclosed a bulky pair of legs with large swelling calves. He had a brown hat on his head, and a pair of scowling eyes, and a beard of three days' growth.

"Come in, d'ye hear?" growled the ruffian. And a white shaggy dog, with his face scratched in twenty different places, skulked into the room.

"What are you up to? Ill-treating the boys, you covetous, avaricious old fence?" said the man, seating himself deliberately. "I wonder they don't murder you. *I* would if I was them. If I'd been your 'prentice, I'd have done it long ago."

"Hush, hush, Mr Sikes!" said Fagin, trembling. "Don't speak so loud."

"None of your mistering," replied the ruffian. "You know my name: out with it! I shan't disgrace it when the time comes."

"Well, well, then, Bill Sikes," said Fagin with abject humility. "You seem out of humour, Bill."

"Perhaps I am," replied Sikes. And then he demanded a glass of gin, adding—"Mind you don't poison it."

After swallowing two or three glasses of spirits, Mr Sikes con-descended to take some notice of the boys. And then the story of Oliver's capture was related by the Dodger.

"I'm afraid," said Fagin, "that he may say something which will get us into trouble."

"That's very likely," returned Sikes, with a malicious grin. "You're blowed upon, Fagin."

"And I'm afraid, you see," added Fagin, regarding the other closely as he spoke, "that if the game was up with us, it might be up with a good many more, and that it would come out rather worse for you than it would for me."

The man started. There was a long pause. Every member of the gang appeared plunged in his own thoughts.

"Somebody must find out wot's been done at the office," said Sikes, in a much lower tone than he had taken since he came in.

Fagin nodded.

"If he hasn't peached, and is sent to prison, there's no fear till he comes out again," said Sikes. "And then he must be taken care on. You must get hold of him somehow."

Again Fagin nodded.

It seemed very important that they should get hold of Oliver again. But, unfortunately, one and all objected strongly to going near a police office to make inquiries as to what had become of him.

And as they sat looking at each other, Nancy and Bet, the two cheerful young women, walked into the room.

"The very thing!" said Fagin. "Bet will go, won't you, my dear?"

"Where?" inquired the young lady.

"Only just up to the office, my dear," said Fagin coaxingly.

Bet said she would be "blessed" if she did.

"Nancy, my dear," said Fagin to the other girl, "what do *you* say?"

"That it won't do; so it's no use a-trying it on, Fagin."

Then followed a lot of discussion. And in the end Nancy at last agreed to go, for, as it happened, she was not so well known at the police office as were the other members of the gang.

So Fagin immediately produced a clean white apron and a straw bonnet for Nancy to wear. "Stop a minute, my dear," said he, giving her a little covered basket. "Carry that in one hand. It looks more respectable, my dear."

"Give her a door key to carry in her t'other one, Fagin," said Sikes; "it looks real and genivine like."

"Yes, yes, my dear, so it does," said Fagin, hanging a large street-door key on the forefinger of Nancy's right hand. "There, very good! Very good, indeed, my dear!" and Fagin rubbed his hands.

"Oh! my brother! My sweet, innocent little brother!" exclaimed Nancy, bursting into tears, and wringing the basket and the street-door key in an agony of distress. "What has become of him? Where have they took him to? Oh, do have pity, and tell me what's been done with the dear boy, gentlemen! Do, gentlemen, if you please, gentlemen!"

Having uttered these words in a heart-broken tone, to the great delight of her hearers, Miss Nancy paused, winked at the company, nodded smilingly round, and disappeared.

"Ah! she's a clever girl, my dears," said Fagin, turning to his young friends.

"She's a honour to her sex," said Bill Sikes, filling his glass. "Here's her health, and wishing they was all like her!"

Meanwhile, Nancy found her way to the police office, where she inquired, with many tears and piteous wailings, as to the welfare of her own dear little brother Nolly.

"I haven't got him," said the police officer whom she addressed.

"Where is he?" screamed Nancy—a picture of distress.

"Why, the gentleman's got him," replied the man.

"What gentleman? Oh, gracious heavens! What gentleman?" cried Nancy.

And then the police officer, pitying the poor distracted sister, told her how Oliver had been discharged because a witness had come up at the last moment and proved that the robbery was committed by another boy; and that the gentleman who had prosecuted Oliver had carried him away, fainting, to his own home; but where that was the police officer could not say.

Nancy wrung her hands, and staggered to the gate. But as soon as she got out of sight of the police court, she ran off as hard as she could to Fagin's, and gave him the information he was waiting for so eagerly.

"We must know where he is, my dear. He must be found," cried the excited Fagin.

Bill Sikes snatched up his hat, whistled to the dog, and disappeared like lightning.

"Charley," said the trembling Fagin, "do nothing but skulk about till you bring home some news of him! Nancy, my dear, I must have him found. I trust to you, my dear—to you and the Artful—for everything! Stay, stay!" he added, "there's money, my dears," unlocking a drawer with a shaking hand. "I shall shut up this shop tonight. You'll know where to find me! Don't stop up here a minute. Not an instant, my dears!"

Then he pushed them from the room, and, first locking the door behind them, he drew from its hiding-place the box of beautiful jewels Oliver had seen that first day.

A noise at the door startled him. But it was only the Dodger speaking through the keyhole to ask whether Oliver should be taken to their other den, if they should catch him.

Fagin answered, "Yes. Find him, find him out—that's all! I shall know what to do next."

The Dodger ran off. And Fagin muttered to himself, "He has not peached so far. If he means to blab us among his new friends, we may stop his mouth yet."

It was just a week since Oliver had left his room. He had grown in Mrs Bedwin's good graces. "A grateful, affectionate child," she called him. And Oliver felt he could have done anything for this good woman—the kindest he had ever met in his life.

Mr Brownlow sent for him one evening, and talked to him very kindly, too; and told him that he was willing and anxious to help him in his future life. "You need not be afraid of my deserting you," he said, "unless you give me cause. I have been deceived before," added the old gentleman, "in the objects whom I have tried to benefit. But I feel strongly inclined to trust you, nevertheless." And then he asked Oliver to tell him his story, and to speak the truth.

Oliver had just begun to tell him about Mrs Mann's baby farm, and Mr Bumble, and the workhouse, when another old gentleman suddenly appeared on a visit to Mr Brownlow. His name was Mr Grimwig.

"This is young Oliver Twist, whom we were speaking about," said Mr Brownlow.

"How are you, boy?" said Mr Grimwig, after staring hard at Oliver. He looked a suspicious old gentleman. He had heard, of course, that Mr Brownlow had brought Oliver away from the police court.

"A great deal better, thank you, sir," replied Oliver.

The old gentleman looked more suspicious than ever; so Mr

Brownlow told Oliver to step down and tell Mrs Bedwin that they were ready for tea.

And Mr Grimwig took the opportunity to hint that Mr Brownlow's goodness would be wasted on the boy.

Mr Brownlow immediately took Oliver's part. And because Mr Grimwig was an aggravating old gentleman, and a very contradictory one, he at once declared that Oliver would deceive his good friend one day.

Now, while they were talking, a parcel of books was brought in by Mrs Bedwin, that had just come from the bookseller's.

"Stop the boy, Mrs Bedwin!" said Mr Brownlow; "there are some books to be taken back."

But the boy had gone. And though Oliver ran one way and the servant ran another, to call him back, they could not find him.

"Dear me, I am very sorry for that," exclaimed Mr Brownlow. "I particularly wished those books to be returned tonight."

"Send Oliver with them," said Mr Grimwig, with an ironical smile. "He will be sure to deliver them safely, you know."

And Oliver, delighted to be of use, said, "I'll run all the way, sir."

Mr Brownlow was going to say No, when Mr Grimwig coughed aggravatingly, as much as to say he would not trust him.

"You shall go, my dear," said Mr Brownlow. "The books are on a chair by my table. Fetch them down."

Oliver brought down the books under his arm, and waited, cap in hand, to hear what message he had to take.

"You are to say," said Mr Brownlow, glancing steadily at Mr Grimwig, "that you have brought these books back; and that you have come to pay the four pound ten I owe him. This is a five-pound note; so you will have to bring me back ten shillings change."

"I won't be ten minutes, sir," said Oliver eagerly. And he buttoned up the bank-note in his jacket pocket, and carried the books under his arm.

Mrs Bedwin followed him to the street door, giving him many directions about the nearest way, and the name of the bookseller, and told him also to be sure and not take cold.

"Bless his sweet face," said the old woman, looking after him. "I can't bear, somehow, to let him out of my sight."

At this moment Oliver looked gaily round, and nodded before he turned the corner.

"Let me see: he'll be back in twenty minutes at the longest," said Mr Brownlow, pulling out his watch, and placing it on the table. "It will be dark by that time."

"Oh, you really expect him to come back, do you?" inquired Mr Grimwig.

"Don't you?" asked Mr Brownlow, smiling.

"No," returned Mr Grimwig, hitting the table with his fist. "I do not. The boy has got a new suit of clothes on his back, a set of valuable books under his arm, and a five-pound note in his pocket. He'll join his old friends the thieves, and laugh at you. If ever that boy returns to this house, sir, I'll eat my head."

With these words he drew his chair closer to the table. And there the two friends sat in silent expectation, with the watch between them.

The gas lamps were lighted; Mrs Bedwin was waiting anxiously at the open door; the servant had run twenty times up the street to see if there were any traces of Oliver. And still the two old friends sat perseveringly, in the dark parlour, with the watch between them.

5

With Fagin Again

Meanwhile, Oliver Twist, having reached Clerkenwell, accidentally turned down a by-street, which was not exactly in his way. He was walking along thinking how happy he was, when he got startled by a young woman screaming out very loud, "Oh, my dear brother!" And he was stopped by having a pair of arms thrown round his neck.

"Don't," cried Oliver, struggling. "Let me go. Who is it? What are you stopping me for?"

The young woman, who had a little basket and a street-door key in her hand, only embraced him, and cried louder, "Oh, my gracious! I've found him. Oh! Oliver! Oliver! Oh! you naughty boy, to make me suffer sich distress on your account. Come home, dear, come home. Oh! I've found him," and she cried hysterically.

"What's the matter, ma'am?" inquired a woman in the street.

"Oh, ma'am, he run away, near a month ago, from his parents, who are hard-working, respectable people; and went and joined a set of thieves, and almost broke his mother's heart."

"Young wretch!" said one woman. "Go home, do, you little brute," said another.

"I don't know her," cried Oliver, greatly alarmed. "I haven't any sister, or father, or mother either. I'm an orphan. I live at Pentonville."

"Only hear him; how he braves it out!" said the young woman.

"Why, it's Nancy!" cried Oliver, who now saw her face for the first time. And he started back astonished and afraid.

"You see he knows me," cried Nancy, appealing to the people around. "He can't help himself. Make him come home, there's good people, or he'll kill his dear father and mother, and break my heart."

At that moment a man rushed out of a beershop, with a white dog at his heels. "What's this? Young Oliver! Come home to your poor mother, you young dog. Come home directly."

It was Bill Sikes.

"I don't belong to them," screamed Oliver. "Help! Help!" and he struggled in the man's grasp.

"Yes, I'll help you, you young rascal. What books are these? You've been stealing 'em, have you?" And Sikes wrenched them from his hand, and hit him on the head.

"That's right!" cried an onlooker. "That's the only way of bringing him to his senses."

Bill Sikes seized Oliver by the collar. "Come on, you young villain," he said. "Here, Bull's-eye, mind him, boy! Mind him!"

Darkness had set in, and it was a low neighbourhood. In another moment he was dragged along through narrow streets. Nancy took one hand, and Sikes held the other.

"See here, boy," said Sikes to the dog, "if he speaks ever so soft a word, hold him. D'ye mind?"

The dog growled and licked his lips. They walked on by little-frequented and dirty ways for full half-an-hour, until they turned into a very narrow street, full of old-clothes shops. And then they stopped before the door of a shop that was closed, and on the door was nailed a board TO LET.

No one appeared to live there. It looked as if the board had hung there many years.

"All right," said Sikes, looking cautiously round.

Nancy stooped below the shutters, and Oliver heard the sound of a bell. They crossed to the opposite side of the street, and stood for a few minutes under a lamp. A noise, as if the sash of a window was gently raised, was heard; and by-and-by the door was softly opened. Sikes seized the terrified boy by the collar, and all three were quickly inside the house.

The passage was fearfully dark. They waited while the person who had let them in chained and barred the door.

"Anybody here?" inquired Sikes.

"No," replied a voice which Oliver thought he had heard before.

"Is the old 'un here?"

"Yes, and precious down in the mouth. Won't he be glad to see you! Oh no!"

"Let's have a glim," said Sikes, "or we shall be breaking our necks, or treading on the dog. Look out for your legs, if you do."

"Stand still a moment, and I'll get you one." And in another moment the Artful Dodger was seen with a tallow candle stuck in the end of a cleft stick.

He grinned at Oliver, and beckoned the visitors to follow him down a flight of stairs. They crossed an empty kitchen; and—opening the door of a low earth-smelling room, which seemed to have been built in a back yard—were received with a shout of laughter.

"Oh, my wig, my wig!" cried Charley Bates. "Here he is! Oh, Fagin, look at him! Fagin, do look at him. I can't bear it. It is such a jolly game. Hold me, somebody, while I laugh it out." And Master Bates laid himself flat on the floor, and kicked in an ecstasy of joy. Then he got up, snatched the light from the Dodger, and, advancing to Oliver, viewed him round and round.

Fagin took off his night-cap and bowed low to the boy. And the Artful Dodger set about rifling his pockets.

"Look at his togs, Fagin," said Charley Bates; "look at his togs. Superfine cloth, and the heavy swell cut! Oh! my eye, what a game! And his books, too. Nothing but a gentleman, Fagin!"

"Delighted to see you looking so well, my dear," said Fagin. "The Artful shall give you another suit, for fear you should spoil that Sunday one. Why didn't you write, my dear, and say you were coming? We'd have got something warm for supper."

At this Charley Bates roared again. And suddenly the Artful drew forth the five-pound note.

"Hullo! what's that?" inquired Sikes, as Fagin seized the note. "That's mine, Fagin."

"No, no, my dear," said Fagin. "Mine, Bill, mine. You shall have the books."

"If that ain't mine," said Sikes, putting his hat on with a determined air—"mine and Nancy's, that is—I'll take the boy back again."

Fagin started. Oliver started too. He hoped the dispute might really end in his being taken back.

"Come! Hand over, will you?" said Sikes.

"That's hardly fair, Bill, hardly fair.—Is it, Nancy?" inquired Fagin.

"Fair, or not fair," retorted Sikes, "hand over, I tell you! Do you think me and Nancy has got nothing else to do with our precious time but to spend it in kidnapping every young boy as gets grabbed through you? Give it here, you avaricious old skeleton. Give it here!"

Saying which, Bill Sikes plucked the note from between Fagin finger and thumb; and, looking the old man coolly in the face, folded it up small and tied it in his neckerchief

"That's for our share of the trouble," said Sikes. "And not half enough, neither. You may keep the books, if you're fond of reading. If you ain't, sell 'em."

"They are very pretty," put in Charley Bates, pretending to read the books. "Beautiful writing, ain't it, Oliver?"

Oliver wrung his hands. "They belong to the old gentleman—to the good, kind old gentleman who took me into his house, and had me nursed, when I was near dying of the fever. Oh, pray send them back! Send him back the books and the money. Keep me here all my life long; but pray, pray send them back. He'll think I stole them. Oh, do have mercy on me, and send them back!" And Oliver fell on his knees at Fagin's feet, and beat his hands together in an agony of desperation.

Fagin looked slyly round. "You're right, Oliver, you're right. They *will* think you've stolen 'em. Ha, ha!" he chuckled, rubbing his hands, "it couldn't have happened better."

"Of course it couldn't," replied Sikes.

Oliver looked from one to the other. No mercy he found in either face. Jumping suddenly to his feet, he tore wildly from the room, uttering shrieks for help, which made the bare old house echo to the roof.

"Keep back the dog, Bill!" cried Nancy, closing the door, as Fagin and the boys started in pursuit. "Keep back the dog! He'll tear the boy to pieces!" And she grasped Sikes by the arm.

"Serve him right," cried Sikes. "Stand off from me, or I'll split your head against the wall."

"I don't care for that," screamed the girl, struggling violently with the man. "The child shan't be torn down by the dog, unless you kill me first."

And as they struggled, Fagin and the boys returned, dragging Oliver with them.

"What's the matter here?" said Fagin, looking round.

"The girl's gone mad, I think," said Sikes savagely.

"No, she hasn't, Fagin," retorted Nancy, pale and breathless. "Don't think it."

"Then keep quiet, will you?" said Fagin, with a threatening look.

"No, I won't do that neither," shouted Nancy. "Come, what do you think of that?"

Nancy looked so ferocious that Fagin, thinking it wiser to change the conversation, addressed Oliver. "Wanted to get assistance? Called for the police, did you?" he snarled. And, lifting a knotted club near the fireplace, he brought it down on Oliver's shoulder, and was raising it for a second blow, when Nancy rushed forward, snatched it from his hand, and flung it into the fire.

"I won't stand by and see it done, Fagin," said the girl. "You've got the boy, and what more would you have? Let him be—let him be—or I shall put that mark on some of you, that will bring me to the gallows before my time."

The men stared at one another in a perplexed manner. Fagin spoke soothingly; and Sikes began to swear. But it had no effect on Nancy in her recklessness and despair. She was not altogether bad, and deep down in her heart she hated herself for having brought poor Oliver back to Fagin.

"You're a nice one," said Sikes presently, with a contemptuous air, "to take up the humane and genteel side! A pretty subject for the child to make a friend of!"

The girl cried out passionately, "God Almighty help me, I am! And I wish I'd been struck dead in the street, before I'd lent a hand in bringing him here. He's a thief, a liar, a devil—all that's bad from this night forth. Isn't that enough for the old wretch, without blows?"

"Come, come, Sikes," said Fagin, appealing to him, and motioning towards the boys, who were listening eagerly. "We must have civil words—civil words, Bill."

"Civil words," cried Nancy, whose passion was frightful to see; "civil words, you villain! Yes, you deserve 'em from me. I thieved for you when I was a child not half as old as this"—pointing to Oliver. "I have been in the same trade for twelve years since. Don't you know it? Speak out! Don't you know it?"

"Well, well," said Fagin, "if you have, it's your living."

"Aye, it is," retorted Nancy. "It is my living; and the cold, wet, dirty streets are my home. And you're the wretch that drove me to 'em long ago!"

"I'll do you a mischief," muttered Fagin angrily. And, as he spoke, Nancy made a rush at him, but Sikes seized her wrists, and, after a struggle, Nancy in her passion fainted away.

"It's the worst of having to do with women," said Fagin,

relieved. "But they're clever, and we can't get on, in our line, with-out 'em. Charley, show Oliver to bed."

"I suppose he'd better not wear his best clothes tomorrow, Fagin, had he?" inquired Charley Bates.

"Certainly not," he replied, answering Charley's grin.

And then Master Bates led Oliver into the next room, where the boys' beds were, and, helping him to take off the new suit Mr Brownlow had ordered for him, Charley Bates tucked them under his arm, saying that he would give them to Fagin to take care of. And, leaving Oliver in the dark, he locked the door behind him.

Oliver heard their noisy laughter from the next room. But he was sick and weary. And he soon fell asleep.

So Mr Grimwig, the suspicious old gentleman, was right, and Oliver did not come back after all.

By-and-by, Mr Brownlow, still anxious for the boy's welfare, and wishing to think the best of him, put this advertisement into the paper:—

FIVE GUINEAS REWARD

Whereas a young boy, named Oliver Twist, ran away, or was en-ticed, on Thursday evening last, from his home at Pentonville; and has not since been heard of. The above reward will be paid to any person who will give such information as will lead to the discovery of the said Oliver Twist, or tend to throw any light upon his previous history, in which the advertiser is, for many reasons, warmly inter-ested.

And then followed a full description of Oliver's dress, person, and appearance; with the name and address of Mr Brownlow at full length.

And who saw that advertisement? No less a person than Mr Bumble the beadle, who had come up to London on a little business for the workhouse.

He read it three times. And in less than five minutes was on his way to Pentonville; and he had no sooner mentioned Oliver's name, than he was ushered immediately into the little study where sat Mr Brownlow and his suspicious friend Mr Grimwig, with decanters and glasses before them.

Both the old gentlemen were very much excited, and soon Mr Bumble was, much to his satisfaction, recounting all he knew of Oliver's life—a foundling, born in the workhouse of low and vicious parents, as he said; that he was also a bad, ungrateful boy, who had run away from his master's house one night, after a cowardly attack on Noah Claypole, the charity boy.

"I fear it is all too true," said Mr Brownlow, very sorrowfully. "I would gladly have given you treble the money if your news had been favourable to the boy."

Mr Bumble pocketed the five guineas that Mr Brownlow laid on the table, and shook his head; and felt very sorry indeed that he had not known earlier that the gentleman would have given three times that amount if he had spoken well of Oliver. But it was too late now.

When the beadle had gone, Mr Brownlow walked up and down, and looked so much disturbed, that even Mr Grimwig forbore to vex him by saying anything against Oliver.

Then Mr Brownlow rang the bell. "Mrs Bedwin," he said, when the housekeeper appeared, "that boy Oliver is an impostor."

"It can't be, sir. It cannot be," said Mrs Bedwin energetically.

"I tell you he is," returned Mr Brownlow. "We have just had a full account of him from his birth; and he has been a thorough-paced little villain all his life."

"I never will believe it, sir," replied Mrs Bedwin firmly. "Never!"

"You old women never believe anything but quack-doctors," growled Mr Grimwig. "Why didn't you take my advice from the beginning, eh? He was interesting, wasn't he? Interesting! Bah!" And Mr Grimwig poked the fire with a flourish.

"He was a dear, grateful, gentle child, sir," retorted Mrs Bedwin indignantly. "I know what children are, sir; and have done these forty years!"

"Silence!" said Mr Brownlow. "Never let me hear the boy's name again. I rang to tell you that. Never. Never on any pretence, mind. You may leave the room, Mrs Bedwin. Remember! I am in earnest."

Mrs Bedwin's heart was sorrowful that night, and Mr Brownlow's heart was sorrowful too.

6

Fagin's Warning

The next day, when the Dodger and Charley Bates went out on a pickpocketing expedition, Fagin took the opportunity of reading Oliver a long lecture. The child's blood ran cold as he listened to his dark threats; and, as he glanced timidly up and met Fagin's searching gaze, he felt that his pale face and trembling limbs were neither unnoticed nor unrelished by that wary old villain.

Then Fagin smiled, and, patting Oliver on the head, said that he saw plainly they would become good friends yet. And, putting on an old, battered greatcoat, he went out, locking the door behind him.

For many days Oliver remained locked up. He could wander about the dirty, empty house; but he never had a chance of getting into the street. How often he thought of his good, kind friends; and what bitter tears he shed when he remembered that they must think him nothing but a thief.

Often he was left alone all day, and sometimes half the night, while the thieves pursued their usual occupations. Spiders had built their webs in the dark corners of the walls, and when he walked softly into a room, the mice would scamper across the floor, and run terrified to their holes.

So lonely was he sometimes, that he would crouch in the passage by the street door to be as near to living people as he could; and he would remain there, listening, until Fagin or the boys returned.

One afternoon the Dodger sat smoking at the table, while Oliver cleaned the Dodger's boots. The child was only too glad to have something to do; and he was so much alone, that it was almost a pleasure to him to have the boys with him, and to hear them talk.

"A pity it is he isn't a prig!" said the Dodger to Charley Bates.

"Ah!" said Charley, "he don't know what's good for him."

And then the Dodger said he would scorn to be anything but a thief. "I'm a prig. So's Charley. So's Fagin. So's Sikes. So's Nancy. So's Bet. So we all are, down to the dog. And the dog's the cunningest one of the lot!"

"And the least given to peaching," added Charley Bates.

"He wouldn't so much as bark in a witness-box, for fear of committing himself; no, not if you tied him up in one, and left him there without wittles for a fortnight," said the Dodger.

"Not a bit of it," observed Charley. "Why don't you put yourself under Fagin, Oliver?" he urged.

"I don't like it," said Oliver timidly. "I wish they would let me go. I—I would rather go."

"And Fagin would *rather* you didn't."

Oliver knew that too well. Fagin feared that the whole gang would be pounced upon by the police, if any outsider could get hold of Oliver to question him. He knew better than to let Oliver go.

"Why, where's your spirit?" asked the Dodger. "Don't you take any pride out of yourself? Would you go and be dependent on your friends?"

"That's too mean, that is," said Charley Bates, drawing two or three silk handkerchiefs from his pocket, and tossing them into a cupboard.

"*I* couldn't do it," said the Dodger, with an air of disgust.

"You can leave your friends, though," said Oliver, with a half smile, "and let them be punished for what you did."

"That," said the Dodger, with a wave of his pipe, "that was out of consideration for Fagin, 'cause the traps know that we work together. And we might have got into trouble, if we hadn't run. Look here," added the Dodger, drawing forth a handful of shillings and halfpence. "Here's a jolly life! What's the odds where it comes from? Here, catch hold! There's plenty more where they were took from."

And then the boys both began to praise their jolly life, adding that if Oliver would not rob watches and handkerchiefs, others would, and that would do him no good.

"And," said the Dodger, "you've just as good a right to them as they have."

"To be sure, to be sure," said Fagin, entering at that moment. "It all lies in a nutshell, my dear—all in a nutshell. Take the Dodger's word for it. Ha! ha! ha!" and the old man rubbed his hands together, and chuckled with delight at his pupil's cleverness.

After this, Oliver was not so much alone; and the boys and Fagin often played the old game together.

Fagin was kind, too, in his way, and kept on explaining to Oliver all the advantages of his trade. Often, sitting over the fire with the three boys, he would tell them stories of robberies he had committed in his younger days, mixed up with so much that was funny and curious, that Oliver could not help laughing heartily with the other boys.

Indeed, the wary old man made his stories as interesting and as laughable as possible, only for Oliver's sake. "Once let him feel that he is one of us," thought the wily old man; "once let him steal; and he is mine!—mine for life!"

And then, one chill, damp night Fagin went to see Bill Sikes about a big robbery that they were planning at a large country house. The place was barred up at night like a jail, Sikes said, and the only way of getting in safely was through a little lattice window at the back of the house—so small that only a very little boy could manage to squeeze through.

Fagin rubbed his dirty hands together, and, in a hoarse voice, suggested Oliver.

"He's just the size I want," said Sikes, considering.

"And will do everything you want, Bill, my dear," said Fagin. "He can't help himself. That is, if you frighten him enough."

"Frighten him!" echoed Sikes. "If there's anything queer about him when we once get into work;—in for a penny, in for a pound. You won't see him alive again, Fagin."

"I've thought of it all," said Fagin. "I've had my eye upon him close—close. Once let him feel that he is one of us; once fill his mind with the idea that he has been a thief, and he's ours!—Ours for life! It couldn't have come about better!" And, crossing his arms upon his breast, the old man hugged himself for joy.

"And wot," said Sikes, scowling fiercely on him, "wot makes you take so much pains about one chalk-faced kid, when you know there's fifty boys about Covent Garden every night, as you might pick and choose from."

"Because they're of no use to me," replied Fagin, with some confusion—"not worth the taking. Their looks convict 'em when they get into trouble, and I lose 'em all. With this boy, properly managed, I could do what I couldn't with twenty of 'em. Now, when is it to be done, Bill?"

"I planned with Toby the night arter tomorrow, if he heerd nothing from me to the contrary."

"Good," said Fagin; "there's no moon."

"No," rejoined Sikes.

"And it's all arranged about bringing off the booty, is it?" asked Fagin.

Sikes nodded.

"And about…"

"Oh, ah, it's all planned," rejoined Sikes, interrupting him. "Never mind particulars. You let me have the boy. Then hold your tongue, and keep the melting-pot ready, and that's all you'll have to do."

After a little more talk, it was then arranged between them, that Oliver was to be brought by Nancy to Sikes's house the next night.

Then, bidding Sikes good night, Fagin wended his way homewards, where the Dodger was sitting up, impatiently awaiting his return.

"Is Oliver a-bed? I want to speak to him," was Fagin's first remark, as they descended the stairs.

"Hours ago," replied the Dodger, throwing open a door. "Here he is!"

The boy was lying, fast asleep, on a rude bed upon the floor; so pale with anxiety, and sadness, and the closeness of his prison, that he looked like death.

"Not now," said Fagin, turning softly away. "Tomorrow. Tomorrow."

When Oliver awoke in the morning, he was a good deal surprised to find that a new pair of shoes, with strong thick soles, had been placed at his bedside, and that his old shoes had been removed.

His heart beat quickly. The shoes looked as if they were to be worn in the streets. He was to go out at last. And then Fagin told him that he was to be taken that night to Bill Sikes's house.

"To—to—stop there, sir?" asked Oliver anxiously. "No, no, my dear. Not to stop there," said Fagin. "We shouldn't like to lose you. Don't be afraid, Oliver; you shall come back to us again. Ha! ha! ha! We won't be so cruel as to send you away, my dear. Oh! no, no! I suppose you want to know what you're going to Bill's for—eh, my dear?"

Oliver said, "Yes."

Fagin looked at him searchingly. He had hoped that all his cunning stories of adventurous robberies might by this time have fired Oliver with a desire to throw in his lot with the other boys, and share the excitement and fun.

"What, do you think?" inquired Fagin.

"Indeed, I don't know, sir," replied Oliver.

"Bah!" retorted Fagin, angry that the boy should not even guess what he might be wanted for. "Wait till Bill tells you, then."

He would not speak to Oliver any more. He was disappointed in him. He was surly all day. Oliver did not know how he had vexed him.

Then, when night came on, Fagin put on his patched greatcoat, to go out. But before he went out, he put a lighted candle on the table, and said, "Here's a book for you to read till they come to fetch you. Good night."

"Good night," replied Oliver.

Fagin walked to the door. Then he stopped suddenly, looked over his shoulder, and said—shaking his hand in a warning manner:

"Take heed, Oliver! Take heed! Bill's a rough man; he thinks nothing of blood, when his own is up. Whatever falls out, say nothing; and do what he bids you. Mind!" And, with a ghastly grin, Fagin nodded his head and left the room.

Oliver sat trembling after Fagin had left him, wondering what could be in store for him at Sikes's house. Then, to get away from his own dismal thoughts, he opened the book that Fagin had given him to read.

It was the history of the lives of great criminals. He read of dreadful crimes that made his blood run cold. And, shutting the book in an agony of fear, he thrust it from him, and, falling on his knees, he prayed God to spare him from such deeds, and to rescue him from the hands of these wicked men.

He was still kneeling with his head buried in his hands, when a rustling noise aroused him.

"What's that! Who's there!" cried the terrified boy, catching sight of a figure standing at the door.

"Me. Only me," replied a tremulous voice.

Oliver raised the candle above his head and looked towards the door. It was Nancy.

"Put down the light," said the girl, turning away her head. "It hurts my eyes."

Oliver saw that she was very pale, and he gently inquired if she were ill.

Nancy threw herself into a chair, with her back towards him, and wrung her hands. But she made no reply.

"God forgive me!" she cried after a while. "I never thought of this."

"Has anything happened?" asked Oliver. "Can I help you? I will, if I can. I will, indeed."

She rocked herself to and fro, and gasped for breath.

"Nancy, what is it?" repeated the terrified Oliver.

The girl drew her shawl close round her, and shivered with cold. Oliver stirred the fire. Drawing her chair nearer to it, she sat there for a little time, without speaking. But at length she raised her head and looked round.

"I don't know what comes over me sometimes," said she, trying to calm herself. "It's this damp, dirty room, I think. Now, Nolly dear, are you ready?"

"Am I to go with you?" asked Oliver.

"Yes. I have come from Bill. You are to go with me."

"What for?" asked the boy, drawing back.

"Oh, for no harm," said Nancy.

"I don't believe it," said Oliver.

"Have it your own way," retorted Nancy. "For no good, then."

Oliver could see that the sight of his own misery had power over the girl's better feelings, and he thought of appealing to her compassion for his helpless state. He also remembered that it was barely eleven o'clock, and that many people would be in the streets, to whom he might cry out for help. So he stepped forward, and said, hastily, that he was ready.

Nancy, watching him, seemed to read his thoughts. "Hush!" she whispered, stooping over him, and pointing to the door as she looked cautiously round. "You can't help yourself. I have tried hard for you, but all to no purpose. You are hedged round and round. If ever you are to get loose from here, this is not the time. I have saved you from being ill-used once, and I do now," added Nancy, white and trembling. "I have promised for your being quiet and silent. If you are not, you will only do harm to yourself, and to me too. Give me your hand. Make haste. Your hand?"

Then, seizing it, she blew out the light, and drew him after her up the stairs. The door was opened quickly, by someone hidden in the darkness, and was as quickly closed when they had passed out.

A hackney-cab was waiting for them. Nancy pulled Oliver in with her, and drew the curtains close. The driver wanted no instructions, but drove away in an instant, and pulled up his horse at Sikes's house.

For one brief moment, Oliver cast a hurried glance along the empty street, ready to cry for help as they got out of the cab; but Nancy was whispering in his ear that to shout for help would be to injure her; and this she did in such a voice of agony that Oliver had not the heart to make the attempt.

"If I could help you, I would," she added, "but I have not the power. They don't mean to harm you. Whatever they make you do, it is no fault of yours."

And while Oliver hesitated, the opportunity was gone. He was already in the house, and the door was shut.

"This way," said the girl, letting his hand go for the first time. "Bill!"

"Hallo!" replied Sikes, appearing at the head of the stairs with a candle. "Oh! is that you? Come on!"

"Bull's-eye's gone home with Tom," went on Sikes, as he lighted them up. "He'd have been in the way."

"That's right," rejoined Nancy.

"So you've got the kid," said Sikes, when they had all reached the room, closing the door as he spoke.

"Yes, here he is," replied Nancy.

"Did he come quiet?" inquired Sikes.

"Like a lamb."

"I'm glad to hear it," said Sikes, looking grimly at Oliver, "for the sake of his own carcase. Come here, young 'un, and let me read you a lecture."

Then he took the trembling boy by the shoulder, and showed him a pocket pistol, loading it carefully in front of Oliver, and putting the barrel close to the boy's temple.

"If you speak a word," said Sikes, "when you are out of doors with me, except when I speak to you, that loading will be in your head, without notice. So if you *do* make up your mind to speak without leave, say your prayers first. D'ye hear me?"

After that Bill Sikes demanded supper, so Nancy went out, and came back in a few minutes with a pot of porter and a dish of sheep's heads. Mr Sikes made a hearty meal, but it is needless to say that poor Oliver had not much appetite.

Then Sikes drank off a couple of glasses of spirits, ordered Nancy to wake him at five o'clock precisely, and told Oliver to lie down on a mattress on the floor. Then he went to bed himself.

For a long time Oliver lay awake, thinking that Nancy might wish to give him some advice; but she sat brooding over the fire, without moving, till Oliver fell asleep.

When he awoke it was not yet daylight, for the candle was still burning; but Nancy was engaged in preparing an early break-fast.

"Now then," growled Sikes, as Oliver started up. "Half-past five. Look sharp, or you'll get no breakfast?"

Oliver was not long dressing. He ate some breakfast; and then Nancy, hardly looking at him, threw him a handkerchief to tie round his throat. Sikes gave him a large rough cape to button over his shoulders. Then taking the boy's hand, he clasped it firmly, gave him to understand that he had his pistol ready in his pocket, and so led him away.

Oliver looked round for a glance from Nancy, but she was sitting in front of the fire, perfectly motionless.

7

With the Burglars

It was a cheerless morning when they got into the street. It was blowing, and raining hard; and the clouds looked dull and stormy.

Sikes tramped along without a word, holding Oliver's hand. Oliver, it is needless to say, was silent too.

Tramp, tramp, tramp. They had started from the neighbourhood of Bethnal Green, and as they approached the City, the noise and traffic gradually increased. It was nearly seven o'clock when they got into Holborn.

"Now, young 'un, you must step out. Come, don't lag behind already, lazy-legs."

Oliver, between a fast walk and a run, kept up with the rapid strides of the house-breaker as well as he could.

They passed Hyde Park Corner, and were now on their way to Kensington, when Sikes relaxed his pace, and seeing an empty cart coming their way, he asked the driver very civilly if he would give him a lift.

The man told them to jump up, and added kindly to Oliver,

"Your father walks rather too quick for you, don't he, my little man?" for Oliver was breathing fast.

"Not a bit of it," answered Sikes, and by a look he gave Oliver to understand that he had his pistol ready. And then he helped Oliver into the cart, and the driver told the boy to lie down on some sacks and rest himself.

They passed Kensington, Hammersmith, Chiswick, Kew Bridge, and Brentford. At last they came to a public-house, and here the cart stopped.

Sikes jumped down hurriedly, lifted Oliver down with the same warning glance, and said goodbye to the man. Then, after a little more walking, he turned into an old public-house, where Sikes ordered cold meat for dinner. Then Sikes smoked a good deal, sitting silent in the corner, and Oliver, being very tired, fell asleep.

When he woke up it was quite dark, and he found that Sikes had arranged for another lift in a cart going his way. Sikes took his hand and helped him up, and off they started in a few moments. It was very dark and very cold, and Oliver sat huddled together in a corner of the cart.

After a long drive Sikes got down once more, and, after a tedious walk through mud and darkness, he turned into a solitary house, all ruinous and decayed. The house was in darkness too; but when Sikes softly pressed the latch, the door opened, and they went in together.

"Hullo?" cried a loud, hoarse voice, as soon as they had got into the passage.

"Don't make such a row," said Sikes, bolting the door.

"Aha! my pal," cried the same voice. And then he called out to somebody with him to show a light.

The timid group, peeping over each other's shoulders, saw a poor little wounded boy.

A pair of slipshod feet came shuffling along, and a young man, whom Oliver had not seen before, and whom they called Barney, came forward with a candle, and welcomed Sikes.

Sikes pushed Oliver in front of him, and they entered a low, dark room with a smoky fire, two or three broken chairs, a table, and an old sofa. On the sofa, stretched at full length, was a flashily dressed individual with reddish hair, his dirty fingers ornamented with large common rings.

This was Mr Toby Crackit—Flash Toby Crackit, as he was known among the gang; and he was going to help Sikes with the big robbery in which Oliver was to take part.

"Bill, my boy, I'm glad to see you," said Mr Toby Crackit. "I was almost afraid you'd given it up, in which case I would have made a venture myself." And then, staring hard at Oliver, he asked Sikes who that was.

Sikes explained. And then he demanded food to put some heart into them, adding to Oliver, "Sit down by the fire, youngster, and rest yourself; for you'll have to go out with us again tonight, though not very far off."

Oliver did as he was told. He had not yet grasped that he was brought there to help them in the robbery; indeed, nothing had been said to him about the robbery, and he was quite in the dark so far.

He looked at Sikes in mute and timid wonder, and sat over the fire with an aching head in his hands; so tired out that he hardly knew what was passing round him.

The men at the table ate and drank, and Toby, half filling a wine-glass with spirits, ordered Oliver to drink it.

"Indeed," said Oliver, looking piteously up into the man's face, "indeed I..."

"Down with it," interrupted Toby. "Do you think I don't know what's good for you? Tell him to drink it, Bill."

"He had better!" said Sikes, clapping his hand upon his pocket. "Drink it, you perwerse imp! Drink it!"

Oliver drank it in sheer fright, and immediately fell into a fit of coughing, which delighted Toby Crackit and Barney, and even made Sikes smile.

After that the men stretched themselves on the chairs, and tried to sleep. Nobody stirred but Barney, who rose now and then to put coal on the fire. Oliver fell into a heavy doze, when he was roused by Toby Crackit jumping up and declaring that it was half-past one.

In an instant the other two men were on their feet, and busily engaged in their preparations. Sikes and Toby put on their great-coats, and buried their necks and chins in large dark shawls.

Barney produced a pair of pistols, which Toby stowed away. They also provided themselves with keys, a small crowbar, and other instruments for forcing locks, while Barney buttoned Oliver's cape.

"Now then," said Sikes, holding out his hand.

Oliver, who was half stupefied with the gin he had swallowed, put his hand into that of Sikes, who told Toby to take the boy's other hand. Barney went to the door and peeped out to see that no one was lurking about; and then the two robbers went into the black night with Oliver between them.

It was pitch dark, and very cold. They crossed the bridge, and soon arrived at the town of Chertsey.

"Slap through the town," whispered Sikes. "There'll be nobody in the way tonight to see us."

Toby agreed; and they hurried through the main street of the little town, which at that late hour was quite deserted. As they cleared the town, the church clock struck two.

Then they turned up a road upon the left hand, and after walking about a quarter of a mile, they stopped before a detached house surrounded by a wall. Toby Crackit climbed the wall in a twinkling, and whispered to Sikes to hoist up the boy.

Sikes had him over in a trice, and the next moment climbed over himself. And then they all stole cautiously towards the house.

And now, for the first time, the terrified boy saw that housebreaking and robbery—perhaps murder—were the objects of the expedition. He gave a little cry of horror; the cold sweat stood upon his ashy face; his limbs failed him; and he fell on his knees.

"Get up," muttered Sikes, trembling with rage, and drawing the pistol from his pocket. "Get up, or I'll strew your brains upon the grass!"

"Oh! for God's sake, let me go!" cried Oliver. "Let me run away, and die in the fields! I will never come near London again; never, never! Oh, pray, have mercy on me, and do not make me steal. For the love of God, have mercy on me!"

Sikes swore a dreadful oath, and had cocked his pistol, when Toby, striking it out of his grasp, placed his hand on the boy's mouth, and dragged him to the house, saying that the pistol shot would make a noise, and that—if it were necessary—he could easily finish Oliver with a crack on the head.

"Here, Bill, wrench the shutter open," added Toby. "He's game enough now, I'll engage."

Sikes, vowing vengeance on Fagin for having sent a boy like Oliver on such an important piece of work, was now plying the crowbar deftly with very little noise, and with the assistance of Toby, the shutter swung open on its hinges.

It was a little lattice window, about five and a half feet from the ground, belonging to the scullery; the opening was very small—just big enough to admit a boy of Oliver's size. In a minute or two, Sikes, with the help of the instruments he had brought, had the window open.

"Now listen, you young limb," whispered Sikes, drawing a dark lantern from his pocket, and throwing the glare full on Oliver's face; "I'm a-going to put you through there. Take this light; go softly up the steps straight afore you, and along the little hall to the street door; unfasten it, and let us in."

"There's a bolt at the top you won't be able to reach," put in Toby. "Stand upon one of the hall chairs. There are three there, Bill," added Toby, who for weeks past had been hanging round the place, finding out all he could—"three with a jolly large blue unicorn and gold pitchfork on 'em—which is the old lady's arms." And then he added, with a noiseless laugh, that Barney had enticed the dog away the night before.

Sikes ordered him sternly to be silent, and to set to work. So Toby immediately made a back for Sikes, who mounted him, and contrived to put Oliver gently through the window with his feet first, and, still holding on to his collar, planted him safely on the floor inside.

"Take this lantern," said Sikes, looking into the room. "You see the stairs afore you?"

Oliver, more dead than alive, gasped out, "Yes." Sikes pointed to the street door with the pistol barrel, and advised him to take notice that he was within shot all the way; and that if he faltered, he would fall dead that instant.

"It's done in a minute," whispered Sikes. "Directly I leave go of you, do your work. Hark!"

"What's that?" whispered Toby.

They listened intently.

"Nothing," said Sikes, releasing his hold of Oliver. "Now."

In the short time he had had to collect his senses, Oliver made up his mind that whether he died in the attempt or not, he would make one effort to dart up the stairs from the hall and alarm the family. Filled with this idea, he advanced at once, though stealthily.

"Come back!" suddenly cried Sikes, quite loud. "Back! Back!"

Oliver was so scared by the loud voice breaking on the stillness, and a loud cry that followed, that he let his lantern fall, and knew not whether to advance or to fly.

The cry was repeated; a light appeared; a vision of two terrified, half-dressed men at the top of the stairs swam before his eyes; a flash—a loud noise—a smoke—a crash somewhere—and Oliver staggered back.

Sikes had disappeared for an instant. But he was up again, and had Oliver by the collar before the smoke cleared away. He fired his own pistol after the men, who were already retreating; and dragged the boy up.

"Clasp your arm tighter," said Sikes, as he drew him through the window. "Give me a shawl here. They've hit him. Quick! How the boy bleeds!"

Then came the loud ringing of a bell, the noise of firearms, and the shouts of the men. Oliver felt himself being carried along at a rapid pace. And then a cold deadly feeling crept over the boy's heart. Oliver had fainted.

"Wolves tear your throats!" muttered Sikes—flying along like the wind, with Oliver on his back. "I wish I was among some of you. You'd howl the hoarser for it."

The shouting of men rang through the air, and the barking of neighbouring dogs, roused by the sound of the alarm bell, resounded in every direction.

Sikes turned his head to look back at his pursuers; but there was little to be made out in the mist and darkness.

"Stop, you cowardly hound!" cried the robber, shouting after Toby Crackit, who, making the best use of his long legs, was already ahead. "Stop!"

Toby knew that he was not beyond the range of pistol-shot, and that Sikes was in no mood to be played with. And Toby came slowly back.

"Bear a hand with the boy!" cried Sikes furiously.

At this moment the noise grew louder. Sikes, again looking round, could see that the men, who had given chase, were already climbing the gate of the field in which he stood; and that a couple of dogs were some paces in advance of them.

"It's all up, Bill!" cried Toby. "Drop the kid, and show 'em your heels." And, with this parting advice, Mr Crackit fairly turned tail, and darted off at full speed.

Sikes clenched his teeth; laid down the body of the wounded boy; threw over the helpless form of Oliver the cape in which he had been hurriedly muffled; ran along the front of the hedge, as if to take the attention of those behind from the spot where the boy lay, and whirling his pistol high into the air, he cleared the hedge at a bound, and was gone.

Three men, who had by this time advanced some distance into the field, stopped to take counsel together. The two first were the butler and footman of the lady whom Sikes had attempted to rob; the third man was a travelling tinker, who had been sleeping in an outhouse that night, and had been roused by the other men to join in the pursuit.

They had been very brave up to this; but when they saw the burly form of the house-breaker bound over the hedge, whirling his pistol in the air, their blood suddenly cooled, and Giles the butler, stopping short, said in a tremulous voice:

"My advice—or, leastways, I should say my orders—is that we 'mediately go home again."

"I am agreeable to anything that is agreeable to Mr Giles," said Brittles the footman, who was very pale in the face.

"I shouldn't wish to appear ill-mannered, gentlemen," answered the tinker. "Mr Giles ought to know."

"Certainly," replied Brittles. "And whatever Mr Giles says, it isn't our place to contradict him. I know my sitiwation." And the footman's teeth chattered as he spoke.

"You are afraid, Brittles," said Mr Giles.

"I ain't," said Brittles.

"You are," said Giles.

"I'll tell you what it is, gentlemen," said the tinker—"we're all afraid."

"Speak for yourself, sir," said Mr Giles, who was the palest of the party.

"So I do," replied the tinker. "It's natural and proper to be afraid under the circumstances. *I* am."

"So am I," said Brittles. "Only there's no call to tell a man he is, so bounceably."

This frank speaking softened Mr Giles, who at once owned that *he* was afraid. Upon which they all three faced about, and ran back as hard as they could.

"But it's wonderful," said Mr Giles, when he found himself at home, "what a man will do when his blood is up. I should have committed murder—I know I should—if we'd caught one of them rascals."

8

At Mrs Maylie's

The air grew colder as day came on. Oliver still lay motionless on the spot where Sikes had left him. Morning came, and with it rain, heavy rain. But Oliver, helpless and insensible, did not feel it.

At last, with a low cry of pain, the boy awoke. His left arm hung useless at his side, and the shawl in which it was wrapped was soaked with blood.

Wondering what the matter was, Oliver tried to rise; but he was trembling in every limb, and fell down like a log. But by-and-by, feeling that if he lay there he must surely die, Oliver made another effort, and, staggering and stumbling, moved slowly on, he knew not where.

And now, bewildering and confused ideas came crowding into his mind. He thought he was still walking with Sikes; he fancied he still heard Toby talking. Then he heard, as in a dream, the sound of shots; the shouts and cries, the noise and tumult, as Sikes carried him away; and with it all, he had an uneasy feeling of pain, which wearied and tormented him incessantly.

Then he staggered on till he found himself on the road. And now the rain began to fall so heavily that it roused him.

He looked about and saw a house not very far off, and bent his faltering steps towards it, thinking that the people living there might have compassion on his wretched condition.

As he drew nearer, a feeling came over him that he had seen the place before. That garden wall! On the grass inside he had fallen on his knees last night, and prayed the two men's mercy. It was the very house they had attempted to rob!

Oliver was so much frightened when he remembered that, that he would have run away. Run! he could scarcely stand! And where, too, could he fly? He pushed the garden gate, which swung open on its hinges; tottered across the lawn, climbed the steps, and knocked faintly at the door.

Just at that moment Giles the butler, Brittles the footman, and the thinker were refreshing themselves with hot tea in the kitchen—perhaps to heat up the blood that had grown cold so suddenly in the fields—and recounting their adventures to the cook and housemaid.

"It was about half-past two," said Mr Giles—"or I wouldn't swear that it mightn't have been a little nearer three—when I woke up, and turning round in my bed, as it might be so" (here Mr Giles turned round in his chair, and pulled the corner of the table-cloth over him to imitate bedclothes), "I fancied I heerd a noise. I says at first. 'This is illusion,' and was composing myself off to sleep again, when I heerd the noise once more distinct."

"What sort of a noise?" asked the cook.

"A kind of busting noise."

And Brittles added that it was like the "noise of powdering a iron bar on a nutmeg-grater."

The cook and housemaid cried, "Lor'!" and drew their chairs closer together.

Giles went on, "'Somebody,' I says, 'is forcing of a door or window; what's to be done? I'll call up that poor lad Brittles, and save him from being murdered in his bed. Or his throat,' I says, 'may be cut from his right ear to his left, without his ever knowing it.'"

Here they all looked at Brittles, who had his mouth wide open—a picture of terror.

"I tossed off the clothes," said Giles, throwing away the table-cloth, "got softly out of bed; drew on a pair of. . ."

"Ladies present, Mr Giles," murmured the tinker.

"Of *shoes*, sir," said Mr Giles, with great stress on the word; "seized the loaded pistol that always goes upstairs with the plate basket; and walked on tiptoe to his room. 'Brittles,' I says, 'don't be frightened.'"

"So you did," said Brittles, in a low voice.

"'We're dead men, I think, Brittles,' I says," continued Giles. "'But don't be frightened.'"

The housemaid protested that *she* would have died of fright. And Mr Giles began to hold forth again, when they were all startled violently by hearing Oliver's timid tap at the door. It was still so early, that they could not imagine who could come knocking at that hour.

Mr Giles, looking at the pale faces round him, and very much afraid himself, suggested that somebody should open the door, and he looked at Brittles. Brittles did not answer, and the tinker had suddenly fallen asleep.

Then, after a little discussion, Mr Giles hinted that they should go in a body to the door, to which suggestion they all immediately agreed, and the tinker woke up directly.

The cook and the housemaid, who were afraid to stay below, followed the men. And by the advice of Mr Giles, they all talked very loud to warn the person outside that they were strong in numbers. Mr Giles also suggested that the dogs' tails should be well pinched, in the hall, to make them bark savagely.

Brittles got well behind the door before he opened it at Mr Giles's command; and the timid group, peeping over each other's shoulders, saw—looking up with piteous eyes, too exhausted to speak—a poor little wounded boy, almost unconscious from pain.

The whole company grew wonderfully brave, and Mr Giles immediately dragged Oliver into the hall, Brittles and he recognizing him in a moment as the house-breaker they had shot.

"Here's one of the thieves, ma'am!" shouted Giles up the stairs. "Here's a thief, miss! Wounded, miss! I shot him, miss; and Brittles held the light!"

And the cook and the housemaid rushed upstairs to repeat that Giles had captured one of the robbers.

In the midst of all this confusion, a sweet voice was heard calling, "Giles?" and the servants stopped talking all at once.

"Hush!" said the voice, which belonged to the niece of the old lady; "you frighten my aunt as much as the thieves did. Is the poor creature much hurt?"

"Wounded desperate, miss," replied Giles, with the greatest satisfaction.

"Wait quietly one instant," said the young lady, "while I speak to my aunt."

She tripped softly away, and soon returned with the direction that the wounded house-breaker was to be carried carefully to

Giles's room; and Brittles was to ride to Chertsey for a doctor and a constable.

"But won't you look at him first, miss?" asked Giles, with as much pride as if Oliver were some bird of rare plumage that he had skilfully brought down. "Not one little peep, miss?"

"Not now, for the world," replied the young lady. "Poor fellow! Oh! treat him kindly, Giles, for my sake!"

Oliver was carried upstairs, and by-and-by the doctor arrived.

Mrs Maylie and her niece Rose were at breakfast when he came; and they had asked him to attend to the wounded robber without delay. He was upstairs a long time. They heard the servants running up and down perpetually, and concluded that something important was going on above.

At last Dr Losberne came down. He looked very mysterious, and closed the door carefully.

"This is a very extraordinary thing, Mrs Maylie," said he. "Have you seen this thief?"

"No," rejoined the old lady.

Now Giles was so proud at his having shot a thief, that he had not as yet made up his mind to let his mistress know that it was only a little boy.

"Rose wished to see the man," said Mrs Maylie, "but I would not hear of it."

"Humph!" rejoined the doctor. "There's nothing very alarming in his appearance. Have you any objection to see him in my presence?"

"Certainly not," replied the old lady, "if it be necessary."

"Then I think it is necessary," said the doctor. "At all events, I am quite sure that you would deeply regret not having done so, if you put it off. He is perfectly quiet and comfortable now. There's not the slightest fear, I assure you." And forthwith Dr Losberne led the way.

Stepping before them, he looked into the room, and, motioning them to advance, closed the door behind them; and gently drew back the curtains of the bed.

They had expected to see a dogged, black-visaged ruffian in the burglar whom Giles had shot. And lo! there lay on the bed a mere child, worn with pain and weakness, and sunk into a deep sleep. His wounded arm, bound and splintered up, was crossed in his breast; his head reclined on the other arm.

The doctor held the curtain in his hand, and looked on for a minute or so in silence. And whilst he looked, the younger lady glided softly past, and seating herself in a chair by the bedside, gathered Oliver's hair from his face; and, stooping over him, let her tears fall upon his forehead.

"What can this mean?" exclaimed the old lady. "This poor child can never have been the pupil of robbers?"

The doctor hinted that it was only too likely.

"But at so early an age!" urged Rose.

"Crime is not confined to the old alone," the doctor replied.

"But even if he has been wicked," went on Rose, "think how young he is. Ill-usage and blows, or the want of bread, may have driven him to join with men who have forced him to guilt."

And then, in a burst of agitation, Rose implored her aunt to have mercy on the wretched boy.

"My dear love," said the old lady, "do you think I would harm a hair of his head? My days are drawing to their close; and may mercy be shown to me as I show it to others." And then she asked the doctor what they could do to screen the boy, for a constable was already downstairs.

After a good deal of discussion, they came to the conclusion that they would do nothing till the boy awoke, and could give some account of himself.

"Now I make this agreement," said the doctor, "that I shall examine him in your presence, and that if, from what he says, we judge that he is a real and thorough bad one (which is more than possible), he shall be left to his fate."

"Oh no, aunt," entreated Rose.

"Oh yes, aunt," retorted the doctor. And he went downstairs to tell the constable that, for the present, Oliver could not be moved or spoken to, on peril of his life.

And then the three waited as patiently as they could till Oliver should awake.

Hour after hour went by; and Oliver still slumbered heavily. It was evening, indeed, when the doctor brought the ladies the news that the child was sufficiently restored to be spoken to. The boy was very ill, he said, and weak from loss of blood; but his mind was so troubled from anxiety to disclose something, that he thought it best to let him do so.

Then the ladies accompanied him into the room; and, bit by bit, Oliver told them all his simple history. It was a solemn thing to hear, in the darkened room—the feeble voice of the sick child recounting a weary list of evils which hard men had brought upon him.

Even the doctor was obliged to wipe his eyes at the end of Oliver's story. And then he went downstairs to, as he said, bully Giles and Brittles into thinking that Oliver was not the boy they had shot.

"Tell me this," said Dr Losberne, after he had frightened them enough, "tell me this, both of you! Are you going to take upon yourselves to swear that the boy upstairs is the boy that was put through the little window last night? Out with it! Come! We are prepared for you!"

The doctor, who was generally considered one of the best-tempered men on earth, looked so angry, that Giles and Brittles, who were considerably muddled by ale and excitement, stared at each other in a stupid way.

"Pay attention to the reply, constable, will you?" said the doctor solemnly. "Here's a house broken into, and a couple of men catch one moment's glimpse of a boy, in the midst of gunpowder and smoke. Here's a boy comes to the very same house next morning, and because he happens to have his arm tied up, these men lay violent hands upon him, and swear he is the thief."

Giles and Brittles looked doubtfully at each other, and then the bell rang violently, and Brittles announced, with some awe, that the Bow Street officers, whom Giles had sent for in the morning, had arrived to carry the captured robber off to prison.

The good doctor was rather taken aback at that, and to gain time he was a very long while explaining how the robbery had been attempted to the newly arrived men, who were named Blathers and Duff.

"Now, what is this about this here boy that the servants are a-talking on?" said Blathers.

"Nothing at all," replied the doctor. "One of the frightened servants chose to take it into his head that he had something to do with the robbery. But it's nonsense—sheer absurdity."

"Who is the boy?" asked Blathers, playing with a pair of hand-

Behind him at a table sat the Dodger and Charley Bates; they were playing cards with another member of the gang.

cuffs. "Where did he come from? He didn't drop out of the clouds, did he, master?"

"Of course not," replied the doctor, with a nervous glance at the two ladies, who had come to see the constables. "I know his whole history; but we can talk of that presently. You would like first to see the place where the thieves made their attempt, I suppose?"

"Certainly," rejoined Blathers. "We had better inspect the premises first, and examine the servants afterwards. That's the usual way of doing business."

Lights were then procured, and all the servants conducted Blathers and Duff to the little window through which Sikes had put Oliver.

After that had been thoroughly examined from inside and outside too, they were provided with a lantern to trace the footsteps with, and after that they were given a pitchfork to poke the bushes with.

Then the two men had a long consultation about the matter by themselves.

All this time Dr Losberne was walking up and down very uneasily, Mrs Maylie and Rose watching him with very anxious faces.

"Upon my word, I hardly know what to do," said the doctor.

They were all very much put about that Giles had sent for these Bow Street officers. Without them the doctor felt that he could easily have bullied Giles and Brittles into acknowledging that they had made a mistake in imagining Oliver was the boy they had shot.

Rose suggested that Oliver's story should be told to the men, as he had told it to them. But the doctor shook his head. He said he was probably an old fool for believing Oliver's story; but believe it he did. All the same, he did not think it was a tale that these practised police officers would believe.

"The more I think of it," said the kind-hearted old man, "the more I see that it will occasion endless trouble and difficulty if we tell these men the boy's real story. I am certain it will not be believed. And even if they do nothing to him in the end, still, the dragging it forward must interfere with your kind plan for rescuing him from misery."

While they were still talking, there came a knock at the door, and Blathers and Duff entered.

They were agreed, they said, that the robbery had been attempted by two persons, who certainly had a boy with them, small enough to squeeze through the window. And then they asked to see the lad.

The doctor immediately suggested, looking at Mrs Maylie, that they should have something to drink first.

Rose went to the sideboard very willingly, and the doctor, satisfying himself that the men were about to enjoy themselves, slipped upstairs to his patient.

By-and-by he came down again, and asked the constables to step up to Oliver's room, into which Giles led them with a lighted candle.

Oliver was half asleep and very feverish. The doctor helped him to sit up, but the boy was too ill to be conscious of what was going on around him.

"This," said Dr Losberne, "is the lad, who, being accidentally wounded by a spring gun in some boyish trespass on Mr What-d'ye-call-him's grounds, at the back here, comes to the house for assistance this morning, and is immediately laid hold of by that clever gentleman with the candle in his hand, who has placed this boy's life in considerable danger, as I can professionally declare."

Blathers and Duff looked at Giles, and Giles looked perplexed and frightened.

"You don't mean to deny that, I suppose?" said the doctor, laying Oliver gently down again.

"I'm sure I thought it was the boy," said the frightened Giles, "or I wouldn't have meddled with him."

And when Blathers questioned him, the poor old butler became more and more confused, and at last said he could not swear to him, and did not think it was the same boy, indeed.

Then the constables went down and questioned Brittles, who was just as confused as Giles, and, in the end, the police officers took themselves off with much contempt for both the butler and the footman.

In the end, a neighbouring magistrate was induced to take the joint bail of Mrs Maylie and Dr Losberne for Oliver's appearance, if he should ever be called upon. And the matter then dropped.

But the boy was very ill. Fever and ague hung on him for many weeks; but under the care of these three good friends, Oliver gradually grew better. How he longed to get strong and well, to do something to show his gratitude to the gentle ladies who had taken care of him!

"Poor fellow!" said Rose, when Oliver one day tried to utter the words of thankfulness that rose to his pale lips. "Poor fellow, we are going into the country, and my aunt intends that you shall accompany us. The quiet place and the pure air will restore you in a few days. We will employ you in a hundred ways, when you can bear the trouble."

Trouble! Oliver could have laughed at that. He said that he would water her flowers, and take care of her birds, and run up and down the whole day waiting on her, if she would let him.

And then Oliver spoke of Mr Brownlow, and of the good old housekeeper who had been so kind to him, and said how he longed to see them again, and let them know that he had repaid them ill—as it must seem to them—for all their goodness to him.

Rose said that they, too, had been thinking of that, and Dr Losberne had promised to take him to London to see Mr Brownlow, as soon as he could bear the journey.

Poor Oliver could have cried for joy. But alas! when that happy day came round at last, and he was able to go with the doctor to London, they found Mr Brownlow's house empty, with a bill in the window "To Let."

They asked next door if the people could tell where Mr Brownlow had moved, and they were told that Mr Brownlow and a friend of his, and the housekeeper too, had left England for the West Indies six weeks ago.

It was a terrible disappointment. Dr Losberne was almost as unhappy as Oliver, and in his energetic way he ordered the driver to "get out of this confounded London! And home again straight!"

Oliver, who had never dreamed for a moment of not finding them, was miserably dejected; and the idea that they had gone away with the belief that he was an impostor and a thief was almost more than he could bear.

The unfortunate circumstances made no difference, however, in the behaviour of his benefactors, and in another fortnight they left the house at Chertsey to spend some months at a little cottage in the country far away. But before they left, the plate that Sikes and Fagin had coveted so much was sent to the banker's for safety; and Giles and another servant were left in charge of the house.

9

Fagin's Secret

And now we must go back to Fagin for a bit, and to the old den where Oliver had spent such lonely days.

Fagin was brooding over a dull, smoky fire. He was thinking deeply, with his arms folded on a pair of bellows on his knee, and his eyes fixed thoughtfully on the rusty bars.

Behind him at a table sat the Dodger and Charley Bates; they were playing cards with another member of the gang, Tom Chitling—who had just been released from prison.

Fagin took no notice of them, for he was buried in his thoughts, which were far from happy ones. Though he had not set eyes on Sikes or Toby Crackit since Sikes's departure from London with Oliver, he knew quite well that the robbery they had attempted at Chertsey had failed.

In his pocket was a newspaper with a full account of the attempted burglary and its miserable failure; and Fagin cursed their bad luck over and over again.

Where was Sikes? Where was Toby Crackit? In hiding, of

course, he knew. And Oliver? He grew restless as he thought of Oliver; and he wished with all his heart he had the boy back safe.

A shout of prolonged laughter from Charley Bates roused him from his thoughts, and he entered into conversation with his hopeful pupils—conversation which turned chiefly on the Dodger's luck at cards.

Tom Chitling was not as merry as the others, for he had been losing all the time. There was no standing, he said, against the Artful Dodger.

"Ha! ha! my dear," replied Fagin, "you must get up very early in the morning to win against the Dodger."

"Morning?" retorted Charley Bates; "you must put your boots on overnight, and have a telescope at each eye, and a opera glass between your shoulders, if you want to come over *him*."

Charley Bates was laughing loud; and the others were still arguing, when the street bell tinkled softly.

"Hark!" cried the Dodger. "I heard the tinkler."

He crept upstairs with the light, and returning, after a pause, whispered mysteriously to Fagin.

"What?" cried Fagin, "alone?"

The Dodger nodded.

Fagin bit his snuffy fingers, his face working in agitation all the while, as if he dreaded something, and feared to know the worst.

At length he raised his head. "Where is he?" he asked.

The Dodger pointed to the chamber above. Fagin told him to bring him down; and ordered Chitling and Charley Bates to leave the room.

The man who followed the Dodger was dressed in a coarse smock-frock, and had the lower portion of his face hidden in a large wrapper, which he pulled off now, and disclosed—all haggard, un-washed, and unshorn—the features of Flash Toby Crackit.

"How are you, Faguey?" he asked in an off-hand way. But he looked as if he had bad news, and dreaded giving it. "Don't look at me in that way, man," he went on, as Fagin fixed his piercing eyes on him. And he added, surlily, that he would say nothing till he had eaten and drunk, for he was starving.

Fagin motioned to the Dodger to put food on the table, and waited as patiently as he could while Toby ate. Mr Crackit was in no hurry to open the conversation, and took a long time over his meal. Then he ordered the Dodger out of the room, and, heartening himself with a stiff tumbler of gin and water, he said, "First and foremost, Faguey, how is Bill?"

"What?" screamed Fagin, starting from his seat.

"Why, you don't mean to say?. . ." began Toby, turning pale.

"Mean!" cried Fagin, stamping furiously on the ground. "Where are they? Sikes and the boy? Where have they been? Where are they hiding? Why have they not been here?"

"The crack failed." said Toby faintly.

"I know it," cried Fagin, tearing the newspaper from his pocket. "What more?"

"They fired and hit the boy. We cut over the fields at the back, with him between us—straight as the crow flies—through hedge and ditch. They gave chase. Curse me! the whole country was awake, and the dogs upon us."

"The boy?" screamed Fagin.

"Bill had him on his back, and scudded like the wind. We stopped to take him between us; his head hung down, and he was cold. They were close upon our heels;—every man for himself, and each one from the gallows! We parted company, and left the youngster lying in a ditch. Alive or dead, that's all I know about him."

Fagin stopped to hear no more. But, uttering a loud yell, and twining his hands in his hair, he rushed from the room, and the house.

Now the other members of the gang believed, without thinking very much about it, that Fagin's anxiety to keep Oliver with him, and make him a thief, was merely to keep him quiet, and prevent him from telling tales, should he ever escape again.

But the wily old man had a deeper design than that—a secret that none of the others even guessed. He had learned, by the merest chance, the true story of Oliver's birth, from a man who had seen and recognized the boy from his likeness to his mother, the first day that Oliver had accompanied the Dodger and Charley Bates on their pickpocketing expedition.

This man, who called himself Monks, had sought out Fagin, and learned, to his consternation, that Oliver had been befriended by Mr Brownlow. He then struck a bargain with Fagin, that if Oliver was got back, Fagin should have a large sum of money; and a still larger sum later on, if he should make Oliver a thief.

Learning, too, from Fagin, the name of the workhouse where Oliver was born, the stranger had found his way there, and—by bribing this one and questioning that one—he had secured at last a little gold locket with the name "Agnes" engraved on the inside, which the old pauper woman, who had nursed Oliver's young mother, had stolen from her dead body.

This was positive proof to Monks that Oliver was the child he wanted; and hearing later on that Fagin had kidnapped Oliver from Mr Brownlow's, he became desperate in his anxiety that Oliver should be made a thief, bribing the old man with larger and larger sums.

It was not likely that such a wary old villain as Fagin was going to do Monks's work blindfold. Not he. He would learn the reason why, so that he might, if possible, have a hold over Monks as well.

So he learned that little Oliver was Monks's half-brother; and that, in their father's will, the greater part of his money was left to *Agnes*, the mother of the younger boy, and, failing her, to her child; but only on the condition that *in his youth he should never have stained his name with any public act of dishonour, meanness, or wrong*. If the money failed to come to Oliver, Monks would have it all.

This, then, was Monks's object in trying to make the boy a thief. And Fagin's object was greed, of course—the large sums offered him by Monks, if he, Fagin, should succeed in making Oliver steal.

No wonder, then, that Fagin uttered a yell of despair at Toby Crackit's story, as he rushed out of the house. Avoiding, as much as possible, all the main streets, and skulking through by-ways, he turned at length into a dismal alley leading to Saffron Hill and found his way to a low public-house called The Three Cripples. It was the meeting-place of thieves and bad characters.

The inn was full of people; and Fagin, catching the eye of the landlord, beckoned him out.

"Is *he* here?" he asked.

The man answered, "No."

"Any news of Barney?"

"None," replied the landlord; and he added that Barney was sure to lie close till all was quiet.

"Will *he* be here tonight?" asked Fagin, with the same stress on the second word.

"Monks, do you mean?" inquired the landlord

105

"Hush! Yes."

"Certain," replied the man, drawing a gold watch from his pocket. "I expected him here before now. If you'll wait ten minutes he'll be…"

"No, no," said Fagin hastily. "Tell him I came here to see him, and that he must now come to me. Tomorrow will be time enough."

"Good!" said the landlord. "Anything more?"

"Not a word now," said Fagin, descending the stairs.

He went down the street again, his face working with anxiety, and found his way to Sikes's house, to question Nancy.

Nancy had heard nothing of Bill. She looked very ill herself; and Fagin, trying to rouse her, said, "And the boy, too. Poor little child! Left in a ditch, Nance—only think!"

"The child is better where he is than among us," cried Nancy passionately. "And if no harm comes to Bill, I hope Oliver lies dead in the ditch."

"What!" cried Fagin.

"Ay, I do," returned the girl. "The sight of him turns me against myself and all of you."

This made Fagin very angry. He said, threateningly, that if Bill came home without Oliver, dead or alive, Nancy had better murder Bill, or he, Fagin, would himself kill Sikes.

"What's all this?" cried Nancy, surprised at his working face.

"What is it?" said Fagin, mad with rage, "when the boy's worth hundreds of pounds to me?. . ."

He stammered and caught himself up quickly, and looked frightened and guilty, staring at Nancy slily, to see if she had taken in what he had said in his mad rage.

"Did you mind me, Nancy dear?" he croaked softly.

Nancy had heard quite well, but she was cunning, too. Had she not been his pupil, indeed?

"Don't worry me now, Fagin," she said. "I'm too stupid to listen. If there's anything you want me to do, you had better wait till to-morrow." She resumed her listless air. And the Fagin's further remarks could not rouse her in the least.

He went off by-and-by quite satisfied that she had not taken in what he had let out; and a a piercing wind drove him—trembling and shivering—homewards. He had just reached his own door, and was fumbling for the key, when a dark figure crossed the road and glided up to him.

"Fagin!" whispered a voice close to his ear.

"Ah!" he said, turning quickly round, "is that...?"

"Yes," interrupted the stranger. "I have been lingering here these two hours. Where have you been?"

It was Monks. And he asked for news now, with a sneer.

"Nothing good," said Fagin.

"Nothing bad, I hope?" said Monks, with a startled look at him.

Then they both went in; and held a long whispered conversation about the robbery, and Oliver's having been left in the ditch.

Monks was fearfully excited. He was afraid that the boy had escaped him after all.

"I tell you it was badly planned," said he. "Why not have kept the boy here among the rest, and made a sneaking pickpocket of him at once? You've done it with others, scores of times."

"It was not easy to train him to the business," answered Fagin. "He was not like other boys in the same circumstances. We had enough of it, sending him out with the Dodger and Charley."

"That was not my doing," observed Monks.

"No, no," replied Fagin. "But we got him back by means of Nancy. And since then she has favoured him."

"Throttle the girl!" said Monks impatiently.

"Well, we can't afford to do that just now, my dear," returned Fagin, smiling. "But you want to make the boy a thief. Well, if he's alive, I can make him one from this time. But if the worst comes to the worst, and he is dead…"

"It's no fault of mine, if he is!" interrupted Monks, with a look of terror; and he clasped Fagin's arm with trembling hands. "Mind that, Fagin! I had no hand in it. Anything but his death—I told you from the first. I won't shed blood. It's always found out, and, besides, it haunts a man… What's that?"

"What?" cried Fagin, grasping the coward round the body with both arms, as he sprang to his feet. "Where?"

"Yonder!" replied the man, glaring at the opposite wall. "The shadow! I saw the shadow of a woman, in a cloak and bonnet, pass along the wainscot like a breath!"

Fagin released his hold, and together they rushed from the room. The candle had been standing just where it had been placed. It showed them only the empty staircase, and their own white faces.

"It's your fancy," said Fagin.

"I'll swear I saw it!" replied Monks, trembling. "It was bending forward when I saw it first; and when I spoke, it darted away."

They looked into all the rooms, and searched the passage outside. But they found nothing. The boys in their own room were fast asleep, and so was Toby Crackit.

It was not fancy, however, though they did not know that till a long time afterwards. The cunning Nancy had followed Fagin, and had heard their conversation.

10

The Face at the Window

Meanwhile, Oliver, at the country cottage, with Mrs Maylie and her niece, was having a happy time—the happiest he had ever known. He had lived so long among squalid crowds, and in the midst of noise and brawling, that this was to him another world.

Honeysuckle and roses climbed the cottage walls; the ivy crept round the trunks of the trees; and the garden flowers filled the air with delicious fragrance.

It was a happy time. The days were peaceful and quiet. The nights brought with them neither fear nor care.

Every morning he went to an old gentleman that lived near the little church, who taught him to read better, and to write; and who spoke so kindly, and took such pains, that Oliver felt he could never please him enough.

Then he had his lessons to prepare at home for the next day, and the rest of this happy time was spent in running errands for the ladies, getting groundsel for the birds, and nosegays of wild flowers to adorn the breakfast table. After that there was a little gardening to do, and plants to water. And if the ladies were happy at having rescued him from a life of vice and misery, how much happier was Oliver in trying his utmost to repay them for their gentle goodness to him!

The spring flew swiftly by, and summer came, and the same quiet life went on at the little cottage, till one sad night when Rose was struck down by a wasting fever.

Dr Losberne was sent for. And Mrs Maylie, writing a letter—which she addressed to Harry Maylie, Esquire—told Oliver to run to the village to get it posted immediately. He had done her bidding, and was turning away, when he stumbled up against a tall man wrapped in a cloak.

"Death!" muttered the man to himself, glaring at the boy with his large dark eyes. "Who'd have thought it? Grind him to ashes!—He'd start up from a stone coffin to come in my way!"

Oliver was frightened, and he ran away; but there was so much to occupy his mind with Rose so ill, that he soon forgot the circumstance.

She was very ill. Mrs Maylie never left the bedside of her niece, and Oliver stole about the house in fear and trembling. Dr Losberne, hanging over her, muttered thickly that there was very little hope; and he used the utmost of his skill to ease the suffering girl.

At last she fell into a deep sleep from which she would awaken, the doctor said, "either to recovery and life, or to bid them farewell and die."

They sat listening, and afraid to speak for hours. The untasted meal was removed, and they watched the sun sink lower and lower, till dusk and dark came on. Their quick ears heard at last the doctor's step, and they ran to the door to meet him, Mrs Maylie imploring him in the name of Heaven to tell her all.

"As God is good and merciful," the doctor said, almost weeping himself, "she will live to bless us all for years to come."

Then Harry Maylie, the old lady's son, arrived to hear the blessed news. And everyone could plainly see that he was in love with Rose.

Giles came too, anxious and white; for he loved his sweet young mistress as much as if she had been his child.

"Have you shot anything particular lately, Giles?" inquired the doctor; for he was in a humorous mood, and very happy at the recovery of his patient.

"Nothing particular, sir," said the poor old man, and he coloured up to the eyes.

"Nor caught any thieves?" persisted the merciless doctor.

Giles answered, "None at all, sir," and tried to look grave.

Whereupon the good doctor asked him to step inside with him a moment; and whispered that Mrs Maylie had requested him to execute a small commission in Giles's favour. And informed him that, in consideration of his gallant behaviour on the occasion of the attempted robbery, a sum of five-and-twenty pounds had been placed in the local savings bank for Giles's sole use and benefit.

By-and-by the daily routine of the house went on again, and with it Oliver's lessons. The little room in which he used to prepare them looked into a garden, whence a wicket gate opened into a small paddock, and beyond that wood and meadow land.

One evening, just before twilight came, Oliver sat at this window preparing his lessons for the next morning. It had been a very hot day, and, as he had been running about a good deal, he was tired, and he gradually fell asleep. Then, as if in a dream, he thought, with a pang of terror, that he was in the Fagin's den again. There sat the hideous old man, pointing at him, and whispering to another man, who sat beside him.

"Hush, my dear," he thought he heard him say, "it is he sure enough. Come away."

"He!" the other man seemed to answer, "could I mistake him, think you? If a crowd of ghosts were to put themselves into his exact shape, and he stood amongst them, there is something that would tell me how to point him out."

The man seemed to say this with such dreadful hatred, that Oliver awoke, and started up in fear.

Good Heaven! what was that! There—there—at the window close before him, with his eyes peering into the room, and meeting his—there stood Fagin. And beside him, white with rage, the scowling features of the very man whom he had pushed against in the village—Monks!

It was but an instant—a flash before his eyes; and they were gone. But they had recognized him, and he them. He stood transfixed for a moment; then he loudly cried for help, shouting, "Fagin! Fagin!"

In a moment, Harry Maylie, who had heard Oliver's story from his mother, with Dr Losberne and Giles, was speeding towards the wood in search of the men. But all in vain. They could not find a glimpse of them.

"It must have been a dream, Oliver," said Harry Maylie.

"Oh, no, indeed, sir!" replied the boy, with a shudder. "I saw him too plainly for that. I saw them both as plainly as I see you now."

"Who was the other?" inquired Harry and Dr Losberne together.

There—at the window—close before him, with his eyes peering into the room, and meeting his—there stood Fagin.

"The very same man I told you of, who came so suddenly upon me at the inn. We had our eyes fixed full upon each other. He leaped over just there; and Fagin crept through that gap." And Oliver's face looked too earnest for the two gentlemen to doubt the truth of his words.

"This is strange!" said Harry Maylie.

"Strange?" echoed the doctor. "Blathers and Duff themselves could make nothing of it."

On the next day fresh search was made, but with no better success; and, inquire as they would, their efforts to discover Fagin and his companion were altogether fruitless.

A few days after that, Harry Maylie went away, and when Rose was quite recovered, the little family, with Oliver, went for a time to London.

And while they are stopping at a hotel near Hyde Park, we must go back for a bit to Nancy.

11

Nancy

The conversation she had heard between Monks and Fagin haunted Nancy. She had heard just enough to know that they were very anxious to get Oliver into their hands again, for some bad purpose of Monks; but not enough to know what that purpose was. Monks had spoken with such hatred of Oliver, that the girl trembled to think of Fagin's ever getting hold of the boy again, and wished with all her heart that the child were dead, rather than that he should be captured again.

She was not well, and her conscience worried her. Nancy could not understand herself Her conscience had never troubled her before; but, somehow, since Oliver had been brought back—and by her means—from Mr Brownlow's, something that lay deep in her woman's heart had been stirred at last. Pity for the defenceless child at the mercy of the wily old man; and remorse that she had been the one to bring him back.

His little, innocent, frightened face would not let her rest, and it troubled her conscience often. And now that he had got away once more, she hoped that they would never set eyes on him again. She would rather know that he was dead.

Sikes had found his way to London after living in hiding for a while; but he had come home very ill. Those long tramps in the rain had given him a chill, which had brought on a fever at last; and for weeks he lay tossing on his bed, with no one to care for him but Nancy and the dog.

Fagin took care to keep away—perhaps he was afraid of catching the fever; indeed, he would not have cared if Bill had died, for Sikes knew many of his secrets, and Sikes was a tough customer at the best of times.

But Nancy nursed him through it all. And Sikes, still weak and ill, was able to sit up at last; Then Fagin, hearing of his recovery, thought it high time to make amends for any neglect of the past few weeks.

"What evil wind has blowed you here?" growled Sikes, whose temper had not been improved by illness.

"No evil wind at all, my dear; for evil winds blow nobody any good. And I've brought something good with me, that you'll be glad to see." And then Fagin told the Dodger, who had accompanied him, with Charley Bates, to open the bundle, and let Bill see the good things they had brought for him.

The Dodger immediately did so, and produced a rabbit pie, and half-a-pound of tea; some moist sugar, a pat of fresh butter, a piece of cheese, and a full bottle of spirits, which Charley Bates uncorked.

"Ah! you'll do now, Bill; you'll do now," said Fagin, as the invalid, without a moment's hesitation, tossed a wineglassful of raw spirits down his throat.

"Do !" exclaimed Mr Sikes; "I might have been done for twenty times over, afore you'd have done anything to help me. What do you mean by leaving a man in this state, three weeks and more— you false-hearted wagabond?"

"Only hear him, boys!" said Fagin, shrugging his shoulders; "and us come to bring him all these beau-ti-ful things."

"The things is well enough in their way," said Sikes, a little soothed as he glanced at the table. "But what have you got to say for yourself? Why should you leave me here, down in the mouth, and down in health, and down in everything else; and take no more notice of me all this mortal time, than if I was that 'ere dog?—Drive him down, Charley."

"I never see such a jolly dog as that," cried Master Bates, doing as he was desired. "Smelling the grub like a old lady a-going to market!"

"Well, what have you got to say for yourself, you withered old fence?" went on Sikes.

Fagin made a few excuses for his conduct, adding, "I couldn't help it, Bill. I can't go in for a long explanation before company; but I couldn't help it, upon my honour."

"Upon your what? Here," growled Sikes, "cut me off a piece of that pie, one of you boys, to take the taste of that out of my mouth, or it'll choke me dead."

Fagin begged him not to be cross. And, after a little more squabbling, Sikes demanded some money.

"I haven't a piece of coin about me," answered Fagin.

"Then you've got lots at home," retorted Sikes. "And I must have some from there."

"Lots?" echoed Fagin, holding up his hands. "I haven't so much as would…"

"I don't know how much you've got, and I dare say you hardly know yourself, as it would take a pretty long time to count it," said Sikes. "But I must have some tonight, and that's flat."

"Well, well," said Fagin, with a sigh, "I'll send the Artful round presently."

"You won't do nothing of the kind," rejoined Mr Sikes. "The Artful's a deal too artful, and would forget to come, or lose his way, or anything, if you put him up to it. Nancy shall go and fetch it, to make all sure." And he added that he wanted five pounds.

After a good deal of haggling, Fagin beat him down to three pounds four-and-sixpence. And Sikes sullenly agreed, on condition that Nancy was to return with Fagin that night to fetch it. So Fagin and the boys got up to go, and Nancy prepared to accompany them.

They found Toby Crackit playing cards with Tom Chitling in the old den. And as the former gentleman had just won all Chitling's money, he got up and swaggered out of the room; and Fagin, saying that it was ten o'clock, ordered Tom and the boys off on a pickpocketing expedition.

"Now," said Fagin, when they had left the room, "I'll go and get you that cash, Nancy." But while he was speaking the bell tinkled, and presently the visitor was ushered downstairs. Nancy had never seen him before, and did not know who he was, but she remembered the voice—the voice of the man who had spoken with such hatred of Oliver.

He said he had had good news, and asked for a word with Fagin, and he looked suspiciously at Nancy. Nancy threw him a careless glance, as if he did not interest her at all, and then looked away.

Fagin said he would not keep her waiting ten minutes, and took his visitor into an upstairs room. In a moment the girl slipped off her shoes, and, gliding from the room, ascended the stairs softly and silently.

Listening intently, she gleaned from their conversation that they had found out where Oliver was, the visitor saying that Heaven had gone against him in putting Oliver into the hands of Mrs Maylie, who, he was sure, would give hundreds and thousands of pounds, if she had them, to know who Oliver was. He told Fagin he had found out that the Maylies were in London, with Oliver, and mentioned the name of the hotel where they were staying, near Hyde Park.

And he added, with dreadful oaths and expressions of hatred, that if the boy took advantage of his birth and history, he might harm even the speaker himself.

"In short, Fagin," the visitor continued—for he was no other than Monks—"Crooked as you are, you never laid for anyone such snares as I'll contrive to lay for my young brother Oliver."

Then Monks, getting very wild, said what a game it would be to bring down the boast of the father's will, by driving Oliver through every jail in the town, and getting him hauled up at last for some dreadful crime.

The villains then put their heads together, as to the best way of getting the child into their possession again. And Nancy stole down, trembling and pale.

So white was she that Fagin—having seen Monks off the premises—started back as he entered the room. "Why, Nance," he said, "how pale you are! What have you been doing to yourself?"

Nancy said, as carelessly as she could, that the place was stuffy and close, and urging him to let her have the money, bade him goodnight, and hurried off as soon as she got it.

Sikes was too sleepy to remark on her white, working face; and all next day he was too much taken up with eating and drinking to see that the girl was on the eve of attempting some bold step—a bold step, indeed, and dangerous too; for Nancy had made up her mind to let the Maylies know the danger that threatened Oliver.

Fearing that Sikes might not fall asleep soon enough that night, or that, waking, he might miss her, and want to know where she had been, Nancy put some laudanum into his medicine, and watched him till he lay like one in a trance.

Then she put on her bonnet and shawl, and hurrying along, looking neither to the right nor to the left, the girl bent her rapid steps towards the West End. As she reached the hotel that Monks had mentioned to Fagin, the clock struck eleven.

It was with some difficulty that Nancy got the porter to take up a message to Miss Maylie, but she begged so hard "for God Almighty's sake," that the man consented at last, and came down presently to tell the trembling Nancy she was to walk upstairs.

Rose received her alone, and spoke so gently, and asked so kindly what she could do for her, that Nancy burst into a flood of tears.

"Oh, lady, lady!" she said, clasping her hands passionately, "if there was more like you, there would be fewer like me."

"Sit down," said Rose earnestly. "If you are in poverty or trouble, I shall be truly glad to relieve you, if I can."

"Let me stand," said the girl, still weeping. "Is—is that door shut?"

"Yes," said Rose, recoiling a few steps. "Why?"

"Because I am about to put my life, and the lives of others, into your hands. I am the girl that dragged little Oliver back to old Fagin's, on the night he went out from the house in Pentonville."

"You!" exclaimed Rose.

"I, lady! I am the wicked girl you have heard of, that lives among the thieves, and that never, from the first moment I can recollect, have known any better life."

"I pity you," said Rose, in a broken voice. "It wrings my heart to hear you."

"Heaven bless you for your gooddness!" sobbed Nancy. And then she whispered low—"Do you know a man named Monks?"

Rose said she had never heard the name. And Nancy, very much agitated, but in earnest, too, told her of the two conversations she had heard between Fagin and Monks concerning Oliver.

"You don't mean," said Rose, turning very pale, "that this was said in earnest?"

"He spoke in hard, angry earnest, if a man ever did," replied Nancy, shaking her head. "He is an earnest man when his hatred is up." And then she added that, as it was growing late, she must go.

Rose then begged her to stay—to leave the bad companions she lived amongst—promising her that she would help her to live a better life.

But Nancy shook her head decidedly; though she wept too, saying, "It was too late!—Too late!" and though they were desperate characters she lived amongst, her life was bound up with theirs.

"But what am I to do?" asked Rose. "This mystery must be looked into, or how will your telling it to me benefit Oliver, whom you are anxious to serve?"

"You must have some kind gentleman about you that will hear it as a secret," Nancy said, "and advise you what to do."

"But where can I find you again when it is necessary?" asked Rose.

Then Nancy made her promise that her secret should be strictly kept, and that she should not be watched or followed if she agreed to meet Rose and a gentleman later on.

Rose promised solemnly. And Nancy said that she would walk on London Bridge every Sunday night from eleven till the clock struck twelve.

Then Rose begged her again to think before she returned to the gang of thieves. But Nancy, muttering again that it was too late—and refusing to take a penny of the money Rose would have given her—only sobbed aloud, and turned away.

12

Oliver Sees Mr Brownlow

Rose said nothing of the strange visit to Mrs Maylie that night, fearing that her first impulse would be to confide in Doctor Losberne, who was coming to London next day; for Rose was too well acquainted with the good doctor's hasty temper to trust him with such a secret.

At last she thought she would write to Harry Maylie; and the next morning she was just going to begin her letter, when Oliver, who had been walking about the streets, with Giles for a bodyguard, rushed back to the hotel in a great state of excitement, with the news that he had seen Mr Brownlow getting out of a coach, and going into a house.

"I didn't speak to him. I couldn't speak to him, for he didn't see me. But Giles asked for me if he lived there, and they said he did. Look here," said Oliver, opening a scrap of paper, "here it is. Here's where he lives. I'm going there directly! Oh! what shall I do when I come to see him, and hear him speak again!"

"Quick!" said Rose. "Tell them to fetch a coach. I will take you there myself—directly." Surely Mr Brownlow would be the one to help her in her difficulty, she thought, with a glad feeling of relief—Mr Brownlow, who had been so much interested in Oliver. She made up her mind to tell Mr Brownlow Nancy's story; and waited impatiently to set off.

The coach was procured, and away they went, the child hardly able to contain himself in his excitement.

Rose made Oliver stay in the coach, while she sent up her card, asking if she could see Mr Brownlow on a little business.

And in another moment Rose was conducted in, where she found Mr Brownlow sitting with his suspicious old friend, Mr Grimwig.

She had no sooner mentioned the name Oliver Twist, than Mr Grimwig dropped his book in his astonishment, and fell back into his chair. Mr Brownlow drew his seat nearer to Miss Maylie's, and begged her, in Heaven's name, to tell him what she knew of Oliver's character.

"A bad one! I'll eat my head if it's not a bad one," growled Mr Grimwig.

Rose coloured as she began to relate in a few words all that had befallen Oliver since he left Mr Brownlow's house.

"Thank God!" cried the old gentleman. "This is great happiness to me." And he rushed out to the coach to bring Oliver in.

As soon as he had gone, the suspicious old gentleman—who was in reality quite as happy to hear the good news, though he pretended he was not—walked a dozen times round the room, and stopping before Rose, kissed her in his pleasure.

"Don't be afraid," he said, as Miss Maylie rose in some alarm. "I'm old enough to be your grandfather. You're a sweet girl. I like you." With that the suspicious old gentleman sat down again.

"Send Mrs Bedwin here, if you please," cried Mr Brownlow, as he came in with Oliver.

"God be good to me!" cried the old housekeeper. "It is my innocent boy!"

"My dear old nurse," cried Oliver, springing into her arms; while the good soul laughed and wept upon his neck in turns.

"He would come back; I knew he would," said the old woman, holding him in her arms.

And leaving her with Oliver, Mr Brownlow led Rose into another room, where she gave him a full account of her strange interview with Nancy.

The old gentleman considered that she had acted prudently in not confiding the matter to such a hasty man as the doctor, and agreed that Nancy's confidence should not be betrayed, telling her to break the news cautiously to Mrs Maylie, and that when the doctor came to London, he would tell him what there was to tell.

13

An Old Enemy

In the meantime, who in the world should come tramping up to London but Oliver's old enemy—Noah Claypole, accompanied by Mrs Sowerberry's servant, Charlotte!

They had robbed the contents of the undertaker's till, and had succeeded in clearing off with their booty.

Through the poorest and least-frequented alleys Noah made his way, and stopped, by the merest chance, at the public-house used by Fagin and his gang—The Three Cripples.

Barney was leaning across the bar, and having supplied the travellers with cold meat and beer in a back room, he at once withdrew, and, going into the chamber adjoining, applied his eye and then his ear at a little peephole, cut high up in the wall, through which he could hear the conversation of the new visitors.

Barney had not been there five minutes when Fagin appeared, to make inquiries after some of his young pupils. Barney informed him in a whisper of the suspicious-looking country pair; and Fagin's ear was at the peephole in a trice.

He listened attentively, and, from the conversation within, he soon learned that the worthy pair had robbed a till and had got away with the money.

This was after Fagin's own heart. He rubbed his dirty hands together, and by-and-by entered the room with a low bow, and a very amiable smile; and sitting himself down at the nearest table, he ordered something to drink of the grinning Barney.

"A pleasant night, sir, but cool for the time of year," said Fagin. "From the country I see, sir."

"How do yer see that?" asked Noah Claypole.

"We have not so much dust as that in London," replied Fagin, pointing from Noah's shoes to those of Charlotte.

"Yer a sharp feller," said Noah. "Ha! ha! only hear that, Charlotte!"

"Why, we need be sharp in this town, my dear," replied Fagin, sinking his voice to a confidential whisper, "and that's the truth."

It was an easy matter for the wily old man to enter into further talk with Noah, and then gradually to let him know that he had learned his secret.

Noah was very much frightened at first, and threw all the blame on Charlotte.

"I didn't take it," he stammered. "It was all her doing. Yer've got it now, Charlotte, yer know yer have."

"No matter who's got it, or who did it, my dear," replied Fagin. "I'm in that way myself, and I like you for it."

"In what way?" asked Mr Claypole, a little recovering.

"In that way of business," rejoined Fagin, "and so are the people of the house. You've hit the right nail upon the head, and are as safe here as you could be. There is not a safer place in all this town than is The Three Cripples—that is, when I like to make it so. And I have taken a fancy to you and the young woman, so you may make your minds easy."

After a little more talk, Noah ordered Charlotte out of the room, while he and Fagin held a whispered conversation on the advisability of Noah's joining Fagin's gang.

"What's the wages?" demanded Noah.

"Live like a gentleman—board and lodging, pipes and spirits free, half of all you earn, and half of all the young woman earns," replied Fagin.

Noah had the common sense to see that whether he agreed or not, Fagin had him in his power, because he had found out his secret. So he consented rather reluctantly, on the condition that the work he could undertake must be very light.

"A little fancy work?" suggested Fagin.

"Ah! something of that sort," replied Noah. "What do you think would suit me now? Something not too trying for the strength, and something not very dangerous, yer know. That's the sort of thing!"

"What do you think of the old ladies?" asked Fagin. "There's a good deal of money made in snatching their bags and parcels, and running round the corner."

"Don't they holler out a good deal, and scratch sometimes?" asked Noah, shaking his head. "I don't think that would answer my purpose. Ain't there any other line open?"

"Stop!" said Fagin, laying his hand on Noah's arm, "the kinchin lay."

"What's that?" demanded Mr Claypole.

"The kinchins, my dear, is the young children that's sent on errands by their mothers, with sixpences and shillings; and the lay is just to take their money away—they've always got it ready in their hands; then knock 'em into the gutter, and walk off very slow, as if there was nothing else the matter but a child fallen down and hurt itself. Ha! ha! ha!"

"Ha, ha!" roared the cowardly bully, kicking up his legs in delight. "Lor'! that's the very thing!"

"To be sure it is," replied Fagin. "And you can have a few good beats chalked out in the neighbourhood of Camden Town, where children are always going errands; and you can upset as many kinchins as you want, any hour of the day. Ha! ha! ha!"

With this, Fagin poked Mr Claypole in the side, and they joined in a burst of laughter both loud and long.

"Well, that's all right," said Noah, when he had recovered himself, and Charlotte had returned. "What time shall I see you tomorrow?"

"Will ten do?" asked Fagin. "And what is your name, may I ask?"

"Mr Bolter," replied Noah, who had prepared himself for such a question being put to him. "Mr Morris Bolter. This is Mrs Bolter;" and he pointed to Charlotte.

"Mrs Bolter's humble servant," said Fagin, bowing with mock politeness. "I hope I shall know her better very shortly."

"Do you hear the gentleman, Charlotte?" said Noah Claypole.

"Yes, Noah dear," responded Mrs Bolter.

"She calls me Noah, as a sort of fond way of talking," said Mr Morris Bolter, turning to Fagin. "You understand?"

"Oh yes, I understand—perfectly," replied Fagin, telling the truth for once in his life.

After that, the matter was settled very amicably, on the condition

The jailer nudged him, and repeated what the
magistrate had said.

that Noah then and there should hand over to Fagin the twenty-pound note that Charlotte had stolen from Mr Sowerberry's till.

Noah made a wry face at that. But there was no help for it, Fagin hinting that he was doing a favour in employing him at all, which he would not have dreamed of doing, if he had not been rather short of assistants at that moment.

So the bargain was made, and they parted for the night, on the understanding that Noah was to find his way to the Fagin's den next morning.

Fagin welcomed him heartily when he came; but he looked a little troubled. And then he informed Mr Morris Bolter, sorrowfully, that his best hand was taken from him the day before.

"You don't mean to say he died!" cried Mr Bolter.

"No, no," replied Fagin, "not so bad as that. He was charged with attempting to pick a pocket, and they found a silver snuff-box on him. Ah! he was worth fifty boxes, and I'd give the price of as many to have him back. You should have known the Dodger!"

No wonder the old man looked sad. It was quite true, indeed. The Dodger—the Artful Dodger—the cunning John Dawkins—had fallen into the hands of the police! A policeman had seen him take a handkerchief out of a gentleman's pocket, but finding it to be an old one, the Artful Dodger first blew his own nose in it and then returned it to the owner's pocket. The policeman kept his eye on him after that, and following him in the crowd, had taken him into custody. Then he was searched, and the silver snuff-box was discovered on his person.

"Transportation for life!" said Fagin sadly. "They'll make the Artful nothing less than a lifer. They know what a clever lad he is."

For in those days robbery was punished often with transportation to Botany Bay—near Sydney in Australia—and to Van Diemen's Land, or Tasmania, as it is now called. A notorious robber was even sentenced to be hanged.

While they were talking, Charley Bates walked in with a very rueful countenance.

"It's all up, Fagin," he said. "They've found the gentleman as owns the box; two or three more's coming to 'dentify the Dodger. I must have a full suit of mourning, Fagin, and a hat-band, to visit him in, afore he sets out on his travels. To think of Jack Dawkins— lummy Jack—the Dodger—the Artful Dodger—going abroad for a common twopenny-halfpenny sneeze-box! I never thought he'd a done it under a gold watch, chain, and seals, at the lowest. Oh, why didn't he rob some rich old gentleman of all his walables, and go out as a gentleman, and not like a common prig, without no honour nor glory!"

Master Bates's voice was husky with regret, and he looked so despondent that Fagin, to cheer him, as well as to impress Noah, said soothingly—"Never mind, Charley; they'll all know what a clever fellow he was. Think how young he is, too! What a distinc- tion, Charley, to be lagged at his time of life!"

After a little more talk, which turned chiefly on the cleverness of the Dodger, Fagin said that somebody must go to the police court to learn how the Dodger fared.

"Shall I go?" asked Charley.

"Not for the world," replied Fagin. "Are you mad, my dear? No, Charley, no. One is enough to lose at a time."

"Why don't you send this new cove?" asked Master Bates, lay- ing his hand on Noah's arm. "Nobody knows him."

"Oh, I daresay about that, yer know!" observed Noah, backing towards the door, and shaking his head. "No, no—none of that. It's not in my department, that ain't."

"Wot department has he got, Fagin?" inquired Master Bates, looking at the lanky Noah with much disgust. "The cutting away when there's anything wrong, and the eating all the wittles when there's everything right? Is that his branch?"

"Never mind," retorted Mr Bolter; "and don't yer take liberties with yer superiors, little boy, or yer'll find yerself in the wrong shop."

Charley Bates laughed heartily at that. And Fagin soon let Mr Bolter know that he incurred no danger in going to the police court, as he was not known at all. And partly through his promises, and partly through fear of him, Noah consented at last.

Fagin dressed him up in a waggoner's frock, velveteen breeches, and leather leggings. And, as Noah was as awkward and raw-boned a fellow as need be, Fagin felt satisfied that he would look the part to perfection.

Charley Bates then led him through many winding ways to within a short distance of Bow Street, and promised to wait for him there till he returned.

And Noah, following the directions he had received, soon found himself in the police court amongst a lot of other spectators. He looked eagerly about for the Dodger; but could see no sign of him. Two or three women were brought in for trial first, and then one or two men, who were all committed, and taken away by the jailer.

And then at last an individual—with big coatsleeves tucked half-way up his arms, his left hand deep in his pocket, and his hat in his right hand—came shuffling into the office immediately behind the jailer. And from the description given him by Charley Bates, Noah knew at a glance that this was the famous Jack Dawkins.

The Dodger began by asking in a loud voice why he was placed "in that 'ere disgraceful sitivation for?"

"Hold your tongue, will you?" said the jailer.

"I'm an Englishman, ain't I?" rejoined the Dodger. "Where is my priwileges?"

"You'll get your privileges soon enough," retorted the jailer, "and pepper with 'em."

"We'll see wot the Secretary of State for the Home Affairs has got to say to the beaks, if I don't," replied Mr Dawkins. "Now then! Wot is this here business? I shall thank the madg'strates to dispose of this here little affair, and not keep me while they read the paper, for I've got an appointment with a genelman in the City, and as I'm a man of my word and werry punctual in business matters, he'll go away if I ain't there to my time, and then pr'aps there won't be an action for damage against them as kep'me away. Oh no, certainly not!"

And then the Dodger asked the jailer to let him know "the name of them two files as was on the bench."

The spectators could not help laughing at the Artful's impudence. And the jailer cried, "Silence there!"

"What's this?" asked one of the magistrates.

"A pickpocketing case, your worship."

"Has the boy ever been here before?"

"He ought to have been, a many times," replied the jailer. "He's been pretty well everywhere else. *I* know him well, your worship."

"Oh, you know me, do you?" cried the Artful. "Werry good. That's a case of deformation of character, anyway."

The spectators laughed again, and the jailer again cried, "Silence!"

And then the clerk called for the witnesses. So a policeman

stepped up, to witness how he had seen the Dodger take a handkerchief from a gentleman's pocket, and blow his own nose in it before putting it back; and how he had followed him till he got near enough to take him into custody, when a silver snuff-box was found on him. And then the gentleman that owned the snuff-box came to witness that it was his, and that he had seen the Dodger hanging about in the crowd.

"Have you anything to ask this witness, boy?" asked the magistrate.

"I wouldn't abase myself to descending to hold no conwersation with him." replied the Dodger.

"Have you nothing to say at all?"

The Dodger pretended not to hear, so the jailer nudged him, and repeated what the magistrate had said.

The Dodger looked up as if roused from deep thinking. "I beg your pardon,' he said, "did you redress yourself to me, my man?"

"I never see such an out-an-out young wagabond, your worships," said the jailer, with a grin. "Do you mean to say anything, you young shaver?"

"No," replied the Dodger, "not here, for this ain't the shop for justice. Besides which, my attorney is a-breakfasting with the Wice President of the House of Commons. But I shall have something to say elsewhere, and so will he, and so will a werry numerous and 'spectable circle of acquaintance, as'll make them beaks wish they'd never been born, or that they'd got their footmen to hang 'em up to their own hat-pegs, afore they'd let 'em come out this morning to try it upon me. I'll ..."

"There! He's fully commited!" interposed the clerk. "Take him away."

"Come on," said the jailer.

"Oh, ah! I'll come on," replied the Dodger, brushing his hat with the palm of his hand. "Ah!" (to the magistrates) "it's no use your looking frightened. I won't show you no mercy—not a ha'porth of it. *You'll* pay for this, my fine fellers. I wouldn't be you for something! I wouldn't go free now, if you was to fall down on your knees to ask me. Here, carry me off to prison! Take me away!"

The jailer had him already by the collar of his coat, and was dragging him off, the Dodger threatening that he would make a "parliamentary business" of it, and then grinning in the jailer's face with great glee and self-approval.

But it was his last fling: and the Dodger knew it. He was locked up in a little cell by himself, and had plenty of time to ponder on the long journey before him, and a prisoner's life across the seas.

Noah went back to find Charley Bates, and the two hastened to Fagin's den, to tell him how the Artful Dodger had distinguished himself on his last appearance in public.

14

Noah Plays the Spy

Cunning though Nancy was, she could not help showing her rest-lessness. She remembered that both the crafty Fagin and the brutal Sikes had confided in her when they had hidden things from other members of the gang.

Much as she hated Fagin, she recoiled to think that he should fall at last by her hand, richly as he merited such a fate. But it comforted her to think that the beautiful lady had promised so solemnly to keep her secret; and that she, herself, had dropped no clue which could lead to the discovery of the gang.

But she was very wretched, and often sat silent and dejected, taking no part in the hilarious conversation where once she would have been the merriest.

The first Sunday night after her meeting with Rose, she tried to keep her appointment on London Bridge; but Sikes, though he was quite well now, was in a sullen mood, and wanted her to stay at home. When Nancy persisted in putting on her bonnet and shawl, Sikes got angry, and swore he would have his way, and taking her bonnet from her, flung it on the top of an old press.

"Tell him to let me go, Fagin," cried Nancy, turning to the old man, who was sitting in the room. "It'll be better for him. Do you hear me?"

Fagin looked thoughtful, but did not interfere, as Sikes flung her into a chair, and stood over her.

"Wot does it mean? Wot did she take it into her head to go out tonight for, do you think?" Bill asked him, as Nancy quieted down after a good deal of struggling and pleading.

"Obstinacy. Woman's obstinacy, I suppose, my dear," said the old man.

"I suppose it is," growled Sikes. And then he added that Nancy had been shut up so long nursing him in his illness, that it had worried and fretted her.

"That's it, my dear," murmured Fagin. And he said goodbye. But he was thoughtful, very thoughtful, as he walked home. Nancy had been very strange lately—very moody and silent. And what did she want to go out for, so late, that Sunday night?

The old man, with a dark look, and a threatening motion of the hand, made up his mind that he would set one of the gang to spy on Nancy's movements. Bolter would do. Morris Bolter, his new associate.

"Bolter," he said, drawing up a chair next morning, as Noah Claypole ate his breakfast, "Morris Bolter."

"Well, here I am," said Noah. "Don't yer ask me to do anything till I've done eating."

"You can talk as you eat, can't you?" said Fagin, cursing his young friend's greediness.

"Oh yes, I can talk," said Noah, cutting a monstrous slice of bread. "Where's Charlotte?"

Fagin said that he had sent her out with Bet, as he wished to speak with Noah alone.

"I wish yer'd ordered her to make some buttered toast first," said Noah. "Well, talk away."

"You did well yesterday, my dear," said Fagin. "Beautiful! Six shillings and ninepence ha'penny on the very first day! The kinchin lay will be a fortune to you."

"Don't you forget to add three pint-pots and a milk-can," said Mr Bolter.

"No, no, my dear. The pint-pots were great strokes of genius; but the milk-can was a perfect masterpiece."

"Pretty well, I think, for a beginner," said Mr Bolter complacently. "The pots I took off airy railings, and the milk-can was standing by itself outside a public-house. I thought it might get rusty with the rain, or catch cold, yer know. Eh? Ha! ha! ha!"

Fagin pretended to laugh too. And Mr Bolter, having had his laugh out, helped himself to another slice of bread-and-butter.

"I want you, Bolter," said Fagin, leaning over the table, "to do a piece of work for me, my dear, that needs great care and caution."

"I say," rejoined Bolter, "don't yer go shoving me into danger, or sending me away to any more o' yer police offices. That don't suit me, that don't; and so I tell yer."

"There's not the smallest danger in it—not the very smallest," said Fagin. "It's only to dodge a woman."

"An old woman?" demanded Mr Bolter.

"A young one," replied Fagin.

"I can do that pretty well, I know," said Bolter. "What am I to dodge her for?"

"Not to do anything," said Fagin, "but to tell me where she goes, who she sees, and, if possible, what she says."

"What'll yer give me?" asked Noah, setting down his cup, and looking his employer eagerly in the face.

"If you do it well—a pound, my dear. And that's what I never gave yet for any job of work."

"Who is she?" inquired Noah.

"One of us," answered Fagin.

"Oh, Lor'!" cried Noah, curling up his lip. "Yer doubtful of her, are yer?"

"She has found out some new friends, my dear, and I must know who they are," replied Fagin.

"I see," said Noah. "Just to have the pleasure of knowing them, if they're respectable people, eh? Ha! ha! ha! I'm your man."

"I knew you would be," answered Fagin.

"Where am I to wait for her? Where am I to go?"

"All that, my dear, you shall hear from me. I'll point her out at the proper time," said Fagin. "You keep ready, and leave the rest to me."

So that night, and the next, and the next again, the spy sat ready in his carter's dress, ready to turn out at a word from Fagin.

Six nights passed. At last, on the seventh—Sunday—Fagin came in with an exultant face, and beckoned Noah out.

He took him to The Three Cripples, and made him look through the little pane of glass (through which Fagin himself had spied on Noah) at a woman who was sitting in the next room. It was Nancy. And Noah peeped till he had got her face by heart. "I should know her among a thousand," he said.

They waited till Nancy made a movement, and went out.

Noah then exchanged a look with Fagin, and darted noiselessly after the girl. She looked nervously round two or three times, all unconscious of the spy behind her. But as she went, her courage came, and she made her way to London Bridge.

It was a very dark night; and the lady she had come to look for was nowhere to be seen. Nancy walked restlessly up and down; and the spy slunk at some distance, in the deepest shadows he could find.

At last, a hackney carriage drew up at a little distance from the Bridge; and a young lady, accompanied by a grey-haired gentleman, alighted, and walked towards the Bridge. They were Rose Maylie and Mr Brownlow.

"Not here," said Nancy, meeting them. "I'm afraid to speak to you here. Come away out of the public road—down the steps yonder."

They followed her down the steps, Nancy whispering that she had such a fear and dread upon her that night, that she could scarcely stand.

"You were not here last Sunday night," said Mr Brownlow, who looked at her with pity.

"I couldn't come," replied Nancy. "I was kept by force."

Mr Brownlow asked anxiously if she was suspected of having spoken to Rose.

"No," said Nancy, shaking her head. And then she told them how she had given Sikes a dose of laudanum before she saw Rose last time.

After a little talk, Mr Brownlow said he believed Nancy was to be trusted, and that he would confide to her, without reserve, that their aim was to secure Monks. But if Monks could not be secured, Nancy must deliver up Fagin.

"Fagin!" cried Nancy, recoiling. "Never!"

And she added firmly that, bad as he was, she would never give him up, because she had worked with him, and he had trusted her.

Then Mr Brownlow said, "Put Monks into my hands, and leave him to me to deal with."

"What if he turns against the others?" Nancy asked

Mr Brownlow said that their only object in wanting to secure Monks was to get at the bottom of his secret concerning Oliver; and if they got the truth from him, the others would go scotfree.

"Have I the lady's promise for that?" asked Nancy.

"You have," replied Rose. "My true and faithful pledge."

"Monks would never learn how you knew what you know now?" questioned the girl, after a pause.

"Never," said Mr Brownlow. "The knowledge should be so brought to bear upon him, that he could never even guess."

"I have been a liar, and among liars from a little child," said Nancy, thinking a while, "but I will take your words."

They both promised her again to keep her secret. And Nancy— in such a low voice that the spy had to strain to listen—described to them the situation of The Three Cripples, and the night and hour on which Monks was most in the habit of frequenting it.

"He is tall," she said, "and has a lurking walk; and, as he walks, he constantly looks over his shoulder." She went on to describe his dark sunken-in eyes, and a broad red mark—like a burn or a scald—that he had upon his throat.

At that, Mr Brownlow started, and muttered to himself, "It must be he." And then he told Nancy that she had given him valuable in-formation, and asked what he could do to repay her.

"Nothing, sir," said Nancy, weeping.

But Mr Brownlow and Rose then besought her to come with

them, and let them put her in a place of safety, away from those dreadful companions.

But Nancy's old cry was that it was "Too late! Too late! "And she begged Rose to give her just her handkerchief, so that she might have something to keep that the beautiful lady had used. And, weeping still, she implored them to leave her. Her agitation was so violent that Mr Brownlow immediately drew Rose away.

As they disappeared, the girl sank down upon the stone steps, and vented the anguish of her heart in bitter tears.

And the spy darted away at his fullest speed, and made for the Fagin's den as fast as his legs could carry him.

Two hours later, Fagin, with face distorted and bloodshot eyes, sat crouching over a cold hearth, biting his long, black nails; and on a mattress, stretched upon the floor, lay Noah Claypole fast asleep.

The old man sat without changing his attitude in the least. He was thinking—thinking deeply.

"At last," he muttered, Wiping his fevered mouth as his quick ear caught the sound of a footstep in the street.

The bell tinkled; and Fagin crept up the stairs to let in the burly form of Sikes.

"There!" said the robber, laying a bundle on the table. "Do the most you can with that. It's been enough trouble to get."

Fagin locked the bundle in the cupboard, and did not speak. And he looked at Sikes with his lips quivering so violently, and his face so altered by the emotions which mastered him, that the house-breaker drew back with a look of real fright.

"Wot now?" cried Sikes. "Wot do you look at a man so for?"

Fagin shook his trembling finger in the air, but his passion was so great that he could not speak for the moment.

"Speak, will you?" cried Sikes. "Open your mouth and say wot you've got to say in plain words. Out with it, you thundering old cur; out with it!"

"Suppose that lad," said Fagin, pointing to Noah, "was to peach—to blow upon us all, stealing out at nights."

"I'd grind his skull under the iron heel of my boot," muttered Sikes, with a terrible oath.

"If it was Charley, or the Dodger, or Bet, or..."

"I don't care who," replied Sikes impatiently; "whoever it was, I'd serve them the same."

Fagin looked hard at the robber. And then, stooping over the mattress on the floor, he roused Noah, who got up with a heavy yawn.

"Tell that again—once again just for him to hear," urged Fagin.

"Tell yer what?" asked the sleepy Noah.

"That about—*Nancy*," said Fagin, clutching Sikes by the wrist. "You followed her?"

"Yes."

"To London Bridge?"

"Yes."

"Where she met two people?"

"So she did." And Noah went on to tell the conversation he had heard, the old man reminding him at the last to tell about the laudanum she had given Sikes.

With a fearful oath, the robber started up, and rushed violently from the room.

"Bill, Bill," cried Fagin, following him hastily.

"Let me out," cried Sikes. "Don't speak to me—it's not safe. Let me out, I say."

"You won't be too violent, Bill?"

The men exchanged one brief glance; there was a fire in the eyes of both that could not be mistaken.

Sikes made no reply; but pulling open the door, he dashed into the silent streets.

And the next morning all London rang with the news of a terrible crime. For Sikes had murdered Nancy.

15

The Fate of Sikes

Meanwhile, Mr Brownlow, with the aid of a couple of men, immediately secured Monks, and had him taken in a carriage to his house.

Here he told Monks that he knew of all his villainy; that he knew too who he was, and why he had caused Oliver to be dragged back to Fagin's. And, addressing him as *Edward Leeford*, he asked him if he dared to brave him still.

It turned out then, that Mr Brownlow had known Monks's father, who had been a dear friend of his; that he knew also of the will that left the greater part of his money to *Agnes*—Oliver's poor young mother—and after her to her child. Indeed, the picture of the beautiful lady that had so fascinated Oliver, when he was recovering under Mrs Bedwin's care, was a likeness of his own mother; but, at that time, Mr Brownlow did not know, of course, that Oliver was her child.

When Monks learned how much Mr Brownlow knew (for the old gentleman, in his anxiety, had even gone to the workhouse, and found out how Monks had bribed a woman there, and secured from her the locket that she had stolen from the dead body of Agnes), he gave in at once, and confessed the whole of his villainy; and promised to write down a true statement of the facts, if Mr Brownlow would agree to settle the matter privately, and not bring the law to bear upon him.

The Government offered a reward of £100 for the capture of Nancy's murderer; for Sikes had disappeared. And Mr Brownlow offered fifty more.

The police surrounded The Three Cripples; and later on succeeded in pouncing on Fagin's den, and caught the old man before he could get away.

And where was Sikes?

Taking the dog with him, he had softly locked the door of the room where Nancy's body lay, and, taking the key, had left the house, and walked rapidly away.

He went through Islington; strode up the hill at Highgate, turned down to Highgate Hill, unsteady of purpose, and uncertain where to go.

Then he struck off to the right again; and taking the footpath across the fields, skirted Caen Wood, and so came out to Hampstead Heath; and making for a field, he laid himself down under a hedge and slept.

Soon he was up again, and back towards London by the high road; then back again—then wandering up and down the fields. He could not rest.

He wandered over miles and miles of ground, and still came back to the old place. It was nine o'clock at night when the man, quite tired out, with the dog limping and lame, turned down the hill by the church of the quiet village of Hatfield, and crept into a small public-house.

There was a fire in the tap-room, and some country labourers were drinking before it. They made room for the stranger; but he sat down in the furthest corner, and ate and drank alone, or rather with his dog, to whom he cast a morsel of food from time to time.

Then he left the inn, and took the road which leads from Hatfield to St Albans.

He went on doggedly. But as he left the town behind him, and plunged into the darkness of the road, he felt a dread and awe creeping upon him, which shook him to the core. Every object before him took the likeness of some fearful thing, and that ghastly figure seemed to be following at his heels.

Suddenly he took the desperate resolution of going back to London.

"There's somebody to speak to there, at all events," he said. "A good hiding-place, too. They'll never expect to catch me there. Why can't I lie by for a week or so, and, forcing money from Fagin, get abroad to France? I'll risk it."

Choosing the least-frequented roads, he began his journey back, resolved to lie concealed within a short distance of the City, and then enter it at dusk.

The dog, though! If any descriptions of Bull's-eye were out, it would not be forgotten that the dog was missing, and had probably gone with him. This might lead to Sikes's being taken as he passed along the streets. And Sikes determined to drown the dog.

He walked on, looking about for a pool; and picked up a heavy stone, and tied it in his handkerchief as he went.

The dog looked into his master's face, and something in the robber's look made him skulk behind. And when his master halted at the brink of a pool, and looked around to call him, Bull's-eye stopped outright.

"Do you hear me call? Come here!" shouted Sikes.

The dog came up; but as Sikes stooped to tie the handkerchief to his throat, he uttered a low growl, and started away.

"Come back!" shouted the robber.

The dog wagged his tail, but moved not. Sikes made a running noose, and called him again.

The dog advanced—retreated—paused an instant—turned; then scoured away at his hardest speed.

Sikes whistled again and again, and sat down, and waited in the hope that the dog would soon return.

But no dog appeared, and he started on his journey once more.

In a low, dirty neighbourhood beyond Dockhead stands Jacob's Island, surrounded by a muddy ditch, six or eight feet deep, and fifteen or twenty feet wide when the tide is in, known, in the day of this story, as Folly Ditch—a creek or inlet from the Thames.

In Jacob's Island, the warehouses are roofless and empty; the walls are crumbling down; the doors are falling into the street. The houses have no owners; they are broken open, and entered upon by those who have the courage. They must be reduced to a destitute condition indeed who seek a refuge in Jacob's Island.

In an upper room of one of these houses—a detached house all falling to ruin, but strongly defended at door and window—there were assembled three men, eyeing each other in some perplexity, in a profound and gloomy silence.

One of these was Toby Crackit; another, Tom Chitling; and the third, a robber of fifty years, named Kags—an old member of Fagin's gang.

"I wish," said Toby, turning to Tom Chitling, "that you had picked out some other den when the two old ones got too warm, and not come here, my fine feller."

"Why didn't you, blunderhead?" said Kags.

"Well, I thought you'd have been a little more glad to see me than this," replied Tom, with a melancholy air.

"Why, look 'e, young gentleman," said Toby, "when a man keeps himself so very quiet as I have done, and by that means has got a snug house over his head, with nobody a-prying and smelling about it, it's rather a startling thing to have the honour of a wisit from a young gentleman placed as you are."

There was a short silence. Then Toby Crackit, giving up his swaggering air, turned to Chitling. "When was Fagin took?" he asked.

"Just at dinner-time—two o'clock this afternoon. Charley and I made our escape up the wash'us chimney, and Bolter got into the empty water-butt, head downwards; but his legs were so precious long that they stuck out at the top, and so they took him too."

"And Bet?"

"Poor Bet! She went to see the Body, to speak to who it was!" said Chitling, his countenance falling more and more—"and went off mad—screaming and raving, and beating her head against the boards! So they put a strait-weskit on her, and took her to the hospital; and there she is."

"Wot's come of young Bates?" demanded Kags.

"He hung about, not to come over here afore dark, but he'll be here soon," replied Chitling. "There's nowhere's else to go now, for the people at The Cripples are all in custody, and the bar of the den—I went up there and see it with my own eyes—is filled with police."

"This *is* a smash," observed Toby, biting his lips. "There's more than one will go with this."

"The Sessions is on," said Kags. "If they get the inquest over, and Bolter turns King's evidence, as of course he will, from what he's said already, they can prove Fagin an accessory before the fact, and get the trial on on Friday, and he'll be hanged in six days from this."

"You should have heard the people groan," said Chitling. "The police officers fought like devils, or the crowds would have torn Fagin away. He was down once, but the police made a ring round him, and fought their way along. You should have seen how he looked about him—all muddy and bleeding, and clinging to the police as if they were his dearest friends. I can see 'em now, not able to stand upright with the pressing of the mob, and dragging him along amongst them. I can see the people jumping up, one behind another, and snarling with their teeth and making at him. I can see the blood upon his hair and beard, and hear the cries with which the women worked themselves into the centre of the crowd at the street corner, and swore they'd tear his heart out!"

Chitling pressed his hands upon his ears, and with his eyes closed, got up and paced violently to and fro, like one distracted.

While he was thus engaged, and the two men sat by in silence, with their eyes fixed upon the floor, a pattering noise was heard upon the stairs, and Sikes's dog bounded into the room. They ran to the window downstairs, and into the street. The dog had jumped in at an open window. He made no attempt to follow them, nor was his master to be seen.

"What's the meaning of this?" said Toby, when they had returned. "He can't be coming here. I—I—hope not."

"If he was coming here, he'd have come with the dog," said

Kags, stooping down to examine the animal, who lay panting on the floor. "Here! Give us some water for him; he has run himself faint."

"He's drunk it all up, every drop," said Chitling, after watching the dog some time in silence. "Covered with mud—lame—half-blind—he must have come a long way!"

"Where can he have come from?" exclaimed Toby. "He's been to the other dens, of course, and finding them filled with strangers, he's come on here, where he's been many a time and often. But where can he have come from first? And how comes he here without the other?"

"He"—not one of them called the murderer by his name—"he can't have made away with hisself What do you think?" said Chitling.

Toby shook his head.

"If he had," said Kags, "the dog 'ud want to lead us away to where he did it. No. I think he's got out of the country, and left the dog behind. He must have given him the slip somehow, or he wouldn't be so easy."

The dog, creeping under a chair, coiled himself up to sleep, without more notice from anybody.

It being now dark, the shutter was closed, and a candle lighted and placed upon the table. The terrible events of the last few days had made a deep impression on all three, increased by the danger and uncertainty of their own position.

They drew their chairs closer together, starting at every sound. They spoke little, and that in whispers, and were as silent and awe-stricken as if the remains of the murdered woman lay in the next room.

They had sat thus some time, when suddenly was heard a hurried knocking at the door below.

"Young Bates," said Kags, looking angrily round to check the fear he felt himself.

The knocking came again. No, it was not Bates. He never knocked like that.

Crackit went to the window, and—shaking all over—drew in his head. There was no need to tell them *who* it was. Toby's pale face was enough. The dog, too, was on the alert in an instant, and ran whining to the door.

"We must let him in," said Toby, taking up the candle.

"Isn't there any help for it?" asked the other man in a hoarse voice.

"None. He *must* come in."

"Don't leave us in the dark," said Kags, taking down a candle from the chimneypiece, and lighting it, with such a trembling hand, that the knocking was twice repeated before he had finished.

Crackit went down to the door, and returned, followed by a man with the lower part of his face buried in a handkerchief, and another tied over his head under his hat. He drew them slowly off. White face—sunken eyes—hollow cheeks—beard of three days' growth—wasted flesh—short thick breath! It was the very ghost of Sikes.

He laid his hand upon a chair which stood in the middle of the room, and—shuddering as he was about to drop into it, and seeming to glance over his shoulder—dragged it back close to the wall, as close as it would go—ground it against it, and sat down.

Not a word had been exchanged. He looked from one to another in silence. If an eye were furtively raised and met his, it was instantly turned away. When his hollow voice broke the silence, they all three started. They seemed never to have heard its tones before.

"How came that dog here?" asked Sikes.

"Alone. Three hours ago."

"Tonight's paper says that Fagin's took. Is it true, or is it a lie?"

"True."

They were silent again.

"Curse you all!" said Sikes, passing his hand across his forehead. "Have you nothing to say to me?"

There was an uneasy movement among them, but nobody spoke.

"You that keep this house," said Sikes, turning his face to Crackit, "do you mean to sell me, or to let me lie here till this hunt is over?"

"You may stop here, if you think it safe," returned Crackit, after some hesitation.

Sikes carried his eyes slowly up the wall behind him; rather trying to turn his head than actually doing it. Said he, "Is it—the—the body—is it buried?"

They shook their heads.

"Why isn't it?" he retorted, with the same glance behind him. "Wot do they keep such ugly things above the ground for? Who's that knocking?"

Crackit left the room, and came back with Charley Bates. Sikes sat opposite the door, so that the moment the boy entered the room, he saw Sikes's figure.

"Toby," said the boy, falling back, as Sikes turned his eyes towards him, "why didn't you tell me this downstairs?"

There had been something so tremendous in the shrinking off of the three, that the wretched man was willing to appease even this lad. Accordingly, he nodded, and made as though he would shake hands with Bates.

"Let me go into some other room," said the boy, falling still farther back.

"Charley!" said Sikes, stepping forward, "don't you—don't you know me?"

"Don't come nearer me," answered the boy, still retreating, and looking, with horror in his eyes, upon the murderer's face. "You monster!"

Sikes stopped half-way, and they looked at each other; but the murderer's eyes sank gradually to the ground.

"Witness, you three," cried the boy, shaking his clenched fist, and becoming more and more excited as he spoke; "witness, you three—I'm not afraid of him.—If they come here after him, I'll give him up.—I will. I tell you out at once. He may kill me for it, if he likes, or if he dares; but if I'm here, I'll give him up. I'd give him up, if he was to be boiled alive. Murder!—Help! If there's the pluck of a man among you three, you'll help me. Murder!—Help! Down with him!"

Pouring out these cries, the boy actually threw himself, single-handed, upon the strong man, and, in the suddenness of Sikes's surprise, brought him heavily to the ground.

The three lookers-on seemed quite stupefied. They did not interfere; and the boy and man rolled on the ground together.

The contest, however, was too unequal to last long. Sikes had him down, and his knee was on Charley's throat, when Crackit pulled him back with a look of alarm, and pointed to the window.

There were lights gleaming below; the tramp of hurried footsteps crossing the nearest wooden bridge. The gleam of lights increased. The footsteps came more thickly and noisily on.

Then came a loud knocking at the door, and then a hoarse murmur from such a multitude of angry voices as would have made the boldest quail.

"Help!" shrieked the boy, in a voice that rent the air. "He's here! Break down the door!"

"In the King's name," cried the voices without. And the hoarse cry rose again, but louder.

"Break down the door!" screamed the boy.

And strokes thick and heavy rattled upon it, and on the lower window shutters; while a loud huzza burst from the crowd.

"Open the door of some place where I can lock up this screaming boy!" cried Sikes fiercely, running to and fro, and dragging the boy now as easily as if he were an empty sack. "That door—quick!" He flung him in, bolted the door. and turned the key. "Is the downstairs door fast?"

"Double locked and chained," replied Crackit, who, with the other two men, still remained helpless and bewildered.

"The panels—are they strong?"

"Lined with sheet iron."

"And the windows too?"

"Yes, the windows."

"Curse you!" cried the desperate ruffian, throwing up the sash and threatening the crowd. "Do your worst! I'll cheat you yet."

Of all the terrific yells that ever fell on mortal ears, none could exceed the cry of the infuriated throng. Some among the boldest attempted to climb the water-spout and crevices in the wall, and all joined from time to time in one loud, furious roar.

"The tide," cried the murderer, as he staggered back into the room, "the tide was in as I came up. Give me a rope—a long rope. They're all in front. I can drop into Folly Ditch, and clear off by that way. Give me a rope, or I shall do three more murders and kill myself."

The panic-stricken men pointed to where such articles were

kept. And the murderer, hastily selecting the longest and stoutest cord, hurried up to the housetop.

All the windows at the back of the house had been long since bricked up, except one small trap in the room where Charley Bates was locked, and that was too small even for the passage of his body. But from this the boy never ceased to call on those without to guard the back; and thus when the murderer appeared at last on the housetop, by the door in the roof, those in front immediately began to pour round, pressing upon each other in an unbroken stream.

The tide was out, and his hope was to let himself down in the ditch, and creep away in the darkness and confusion. He set his foot against the stack of chimneys; fastened one end of the rope tightly and firmly round it, and with the other made a strong running noose, by the aid of his hands and teeth, almost in a second.

This he intended to slip under his armpits, and had just put the loop over his head for that purpose, when, with a yell of terror, he lost his balance, and tumbled over the parapet. The noose was on his neck. It ran up with his weight. There was a sudden jerk, a terrific convulsion of the limbs;—Sikes had hanged himself!

The murderer swung lifeless against the wall. And Charley Bates, thrusting aside the dangling body that hid his view, called to the people to come and take him out, for God's sake.

The dog, which had lain concealed till now, ran backwards and forwards on the parapet with a dismal howl, and, collecting himself for a spring, jumped for the dead man's shoulders. Missing his aim, he fell into the ditch, and, striking his head against a stone, dashed out his brains.

16

Fagin's Last Night

Noah Claypole, to save himself, immediately turned informer, and being able to prove that Fagin was "an accessory before the fact"— which means that he had given countenance to Sikes's crime—Fagin was sentenced to be hanged.

They led him through a paved room under the court, where some prisoners were waiting till their turn came, and others were talking to their friends. But there was nobody there to speak to *him*.

His conductors hurried him on, through a gloomy passage lighted by a few dim lamps, into the interior of the prison.

Here he was searched, and then they led him to one of the condemned cells, and left him—alone.

He sat down on a stone bench opposite the door, which served for seat and bedstead; and casting his bloodshot eyes upon the ground, tried to collect his thoughts.

After a while, he began to remember what the judge had said:— "To be hanged by the neck till he was dead." That was the end!

As it came on very dark, he began to think of all the men he had known who had died upon the scaffold—some of them through his means.

Some of them might have been imprisoned in that very cell; might have sat upon that very spot.

It was very dark. Why didn't they bring a light?

"Light! Light!" and he beat upon the door.

Two men appeared; one bearing a candle, which he thrust into an iron candlestick fixed against the wall.

Rabbis came next day to pray beside him; but he drove them off with curses.

Now he had only one more night to live. And as he thought of this, he cowered down upon his stone bed and thought of the past.

His red hair hung down upon his pallid face; his beard was torn and twisted into knots; his eyes shone with a terrible light.

By-and-by Mr Brownlow and Oliver appeared at the prison, and presented an Order of Admission to the prisoner, signed by one of the sheriffs.

"Is the young gentleman to come too, sir?" said the man whose duty it was to conduct them. "It's not a sight for children, sir."

"It is not, indeed, my friend," rejoined Mr Brownlow; "but my business with this man is connected with this child."

At that, the man touched his hat, and led them on, through dark and winding ways, towards the cells.

Fagin was seated on his bed, rocking himself from side to side, his mind evidently wandering to his old life.

They heard him mumble, "Good boy, Charley—well done!—Oliver too, ha, ha!—quite the gentleman! Take the boy away to bed."

The jailer took Oliver by the hand, and, whispering to him not to be alarmed, looked on without speaking.

"Take him away to bed!" cried Fagin. "Do you hear me—some of you? He has been the—the—somehow the cause of all this."

"Fagin!" said the jailer.

"That's me!" cried the prisoner. And he thought he was speaking to the judge. "An old man, my lord—a very old, old man." It had been his answer when the judge had asked him if he had anything to say.

"Here's somebody wants to see you," cried the jailer. "Fagin! Fagin!"

At that, the old man caught sight of Oliver and Mr Brownlow. And, shrinking to the furthest corner of his seat, he demanded to know what they wanted there.

"You have some papers," said Mr Brownlow, advancing, "some papers which were placed in your hands, for better security, by a man called Monks."

"It's all a lie," muttered Fagin. "I haven't one—not one."

"For the love of God," said Mr Brownlow solemnly, "do not say that now, upon the very verge of death; but tell me where they are. You know that Sikes is dead—that Monks has confessed; that there is no hope of further gain. Where are those papers?"

"Oliver," cried Fagin, beckoning to him. "Here, here! Let me whisper to you."

"I am not afraid," said Oliver in a low voice, as he let go the jailer's hand.

"The papers," said Fagin, drawing Oliver towards him, "are in a canvas bag, in a hole a little way up the chimney in the top of the front room. I want to talk to you, my dear. I want to talk to you."

"Yes, yes," returned Oliver. "Let me say a prayer. Say only one upon your knees, and we will talk till morning."

"Outside, outside," replied Fagin, pushing the boy before him towards the door. "Say I've gone to sleep—they'll believe *you.* You can get me out, if you lead me so. Now then, now then!"

"Oh! God forgive this wretched man!" cried Oliver, with a burst of tears.

"That's right, that's right," said Fagin. "That'll help us on. This door first. Now—now—now!"

"Have you nothing else to ask him, sir?" asked the turnkey.

"Nothing," said Mr Brownlow.

The door of the cell opened, and the attendants appeared.

"Press on, press on," muttered Fagin. "Faster, faster!"

The men laid hands upon him, and, taking Oliver from his grasp, held Fagin back.

He struggled for an instant, and then sent up a cry that rang in their ears until they reached the open yard.

Next morning he was hanged.

Charley Bates, appalled at Nancy's murder, came to the conclusion that an honest life was best, and struggled hard to lead a better life. After a good deal of suffering, he succeeded at last in getting honest work in the country.

Monks went to America with the portion his father had left him, but he soon squandered it, and, being taken in an act of knavery, he was sent to prison, where he died.

In prison, too, across the seas, died also the Artful Dodger.

Rose married Harry Maylie; and Mrs Maylie took up her abode with them.

The good doctor missed his friends so much at Chertsey, that he gave up his practice, and came to live near them.

Close, too, lives Mr Brownlow, with Mrs Bedwin for his house-keeper, and Oliver for his adopted son.

The suspicious old gentleman often comes to visit them, and Mr Brownlow loves to joke him on his prophecy concerning Oliver, and reminds him of the night they sat with the watch between them, waiting for his return. Mr Grimwig always retorts that, at any rate, he was right that night, and Oliver did not come back; which only makes Mr Brownlow laugh so heartily, that Mr Grimwig is constrained to laugh as well.

Mr Brownlow teaches his adopted son, and every day gets more attached to him; for Oliver, tried by adversity, remembers its lessons, in love and mercy to others; giving fervent thanks to God who has protected and preserved him, and brought him safe through all.